JEWELL

B.D. Pedersen

Edited by
June Pedersen

Cover Design
Mike Lynam
Red Fence Productions

ISBN -13: 978-0615849348

Prologue

Every year Phil Morles would take his annual vacation in southern California, on the beaches. He loves it down there. Not to live, but just to visit for three to four weeks each summer. Yeah, it may sound boring to you, but for a geek like him, he loved it.

If it was not for the fact that he drove there each year, he would have never met Jewell. In addition, he would have never ended up running for his life three quarters of the way across this country.

It was a mind dulling experience and a life altering process. For one who had never killed anyone let alone held a gun, this experience would be both a blessing and a burden.

It was just a simple rest stop in the northern part of Cowlitz County, Washington.

Phil was southbound on Interstate 5 and needed to use the facilities. How many people do that every day, year around, all over this country? It was just his luck to do it in the one place where Jewell Scarpone happened to be waiting for a ride.

Phil must have been just the right personality type for Jewell because he was waiting at Phil's car when Phil came back out. All Phil's friends and his mother had always told him never pick-up strangers along the road. One day he would pay for it and they did not want to have to bury him because of his stupidity. Boy did he wish he had listened, but that was then and this is now. He lived.

Jewell turned out to be much more than just a stranded person wanting to get a ride to the San Francisco or Los Angeles areas, and hoping that someone would give him that ride. Well that someone turned out to be Phil. Jewell seemed like an all-right guy and right now Phil still feels that way. After running together and fighting together you tend to grow an attachment for a person. Well anyway Phil is loyal to Jewell and that's that.

He had read books on hoods and the mob in the past and they always made the hit-man a real jerk, a blood thirsty, kill crazy animal that lived for the opportunity to kill his next victim. Well, Phil did not believe that, some may have been like that, but not Jewell. Yes, Jewell was a professional killer, but he had ethics as well. Well, Phil felt that he did. On top of that if it had not been for Jewell Phil would have been dead a long time ago.

The man was a machine when it came to gun play. He had more moves than an exotic dancer and when he pulled the trigger, someone was going to come out on the wrong end of living, I mean dying, I mean, well it was going to be bad news.

What Phil did not know was that when he first met Jewell, the game had been playing for a number of weeks, had started in Chicago and had worked its way all the way out here to Washington State. That game would put the whole mob out hunting for Jewell, and now Phil, in retribution for the death of the son of a mob boss back in Chicago. It turned out to have been Jewell's best friend and the boss was his friend's dad. You know a family thing.

Just being with Jewell marked Phil for death; he had done nothing to deserve it just being with Jewell was enough. What started out as a dream vacation had turned into a nightmare, and Phil had no idea how it would come out?

Once into it he had no choice but to join in with Jewell and fight for his life, as best as he could under the circumstances. Wait, why keep playing around with this. Let me tell you just what happened and how the two of them manage to survive the ordeal.

My name is David Spalding and I'm a good friend of Phil's, I am also Phil's attorney. So, the story I am going to relate to you may be considered as a client and attorney thing, but Phil feels that the truth needed to be addressed. I guess the best place is to start at the beginning and then lay it out as it happened. So, put yourself on the Interstate 5 and get ready for a fast run south, under fire.

Chapter One

THE MEETING

Phil met Jewell for the first time at a rest stop on Interstate 5 just a mile south of the Lewis and Cowlitz County's line in southwestern Washington State. He was traveling south, his destination being the Long Beach, California area. He had four weeks of vacation time and he loved the southwest area of the States, especially the beaches. It would take him three days driving to get there, but that's the way he liked it. He had his favorite places to stop at on the way. It was his idea of a perfect vacation.

His name is Phillip Morles and he lives in Everett, Washington about twenty miles or so north of Seattle. Everyone called him Phil for short, besides he liked that name better than his full name. Phil had lived in Everett all his life, attending school and graduating from high school there. He eventually went to the University of Washington and attained his degree in Computer Sciences.

When one would look at Phil, they would see a man around one hundred ninety-five pounds and about six feet tall. He had solid brown eyes and thick black hair. For a guy his age he was not that bad looking, you might even say he was handsome. Yet, he was single and had no children. He had been married for a short time about two years ago, but it hadn't worked out.

One would probably look at Phil and tag him as a geek. You know what a geek is, a technocrat, one who plays, works, or develops computer related technology. He was a computer whiz, in great demand in the greater Seattle area. Based on that description you would never guess this man would become involved in an adventure that would rival even the best of all adventure stories fact or fiction.

Try to imagine two men of absolutely opposite personalities. I mean men who were so different from one another they would never meet at any group gathering anywhere across the nation. Well, that is exactly what was going to happen to Phil in the near future.

He was about to meet a man who would take him on the trip of a lifetime, well maybe it would be more like a trip that could easily end his life. He would start out by making the simplest of decisions and end up fighting for his life across three quarters of this nation. Now that's a vacation.

It was a Saturday morning when he loaded up his car and headed south on I-5, heading out on his annual vacation to his favorite location, Southern California. You would think for the number of times he had taken his vacations in that area; he would just move down there permanently.

But he liked where he lived and the trip to Southern California was a temporary thing and that was the key to it all, temporary. Though he liked the beaches in that area, it was too populated for him. Besides the actual trip south was one of his favorite parts about the vacation.

From Everett south through Portland and down to Salem was much like the Seattle area, lots of urban development and heavy traffic. But once he turned west at Salem and hit the coast Highway 101 it was a whole different game. From Lincoln City south it was like a string of pearls each town a gem of its own. His primary targets on these runs down the coast were the many galleries that dotted the coastal highway.

Following Lincoln City was Depoe Bay and Newport and the Aquarium just south of there. Past Florence, where the great sand dunes on the Pacific Beaches are found, then down through Winchester Bay. From there it's on to Reedsport, Coos Bay and finally Brookings before crossing into California.

He would then continue on to Crescent City and on south on 101 to San Jose where he would cut over on SR-17 to Highway 1 at Santa Cruz. Highway 1 is known as the Cabrillo Highway and it is on this section of his trip, he found the most inviting and restful locations.

Driving through the Big Sur was an experience all to itself. The nature of the towns he would pass through was unique. There was Watsonville, Monterey, and Carmel known for their laid back and private existence with an arts community that few could rival.

From there he would travel on down to San Simeon, Morro Bay, Santa Barbara, and on into the Greater Los Angeles area.

In all that distance he seldom lost sight of the Pacific Ocean for any appreciable period of time. It was always there, off to his right spreading out like a blue blanket. From time to time, it would be broken up by the presence of an island or a ship plying its way toward some coastal port or far off place.

During this time of the year, it was as close to heaven as one could get. The forests would drop down toward the ocean and end at the edge of the cliffs and cling there, as the cliffs drop off toward the water where the land met the sea.

When the weather became angry it would charge into the Big Sur in a suicidal attack that would shake the entire coast line. The Pacific would claw at the land and tear into it slowly pulling the land into the sea in a never-ending process of changing the coastal line. To this the Cabrillo Highway clung to the sides of the Big Sur.

So, there he was traveling south approaching the county line between Lewis and Cowlitz Counties, in Southwestern Washington when that good old call to nature

13

hit him and he decided to take a rest stop just south of the county line. It was that innocent necessary stop which would change his life.

He pulled into the southbound Toutle River Rest Area, found a parking place right in front of the facilities and left his car. The place was fairly busy for this time of day and he was hoping there were not too many in the line.

Rest stops in this part of Washington are multiservice facilities, as are most up and down the west coast. This facility was capable of handling commercial rigs, private trailer, fifth wheel units, and of course cars. It was a gathering place for every type of individual possible and it was in this place two total strangers would meet for the first time.

It only took a few minutes and in complete relief he returned to his car. As he approached the spot where his car was parked, he saw a man standing by the left side rear bumper of his car watching him walk up to the driver's door. Phil looked around to see if there was anyone else with this guy and also to check and make sure there were others close by just in case. In case of what? You know.

He was about five feet eleven, probably

weighed around two hundred pounds. Short cut blond hair and had not shaven in a day or two. He looked to be pleasant and calm, but by his stance he was alert and probably missed little if anything around him. He was dressed casual but neat. There were two suitcases sitting on the ground beside him.

As Phil walked around the front of his car approaching the driver's door the stranger approached him in a relaxed and casual manner, "Hi, how far south are you going?"

Phil was not sure just what to say or how to respond. He knew immediately what this guy was going to ask him. He was not opposed to giving people rides, but here and now and under these conditions, things looked a little suspicious, "The Los Angeles Area." Phil responded.

The stranger stood there sizing Phil up. He was looking for just the right person, one he could tell his story to and would not have too many questions and right then Phil appeared to fit the bill. He then asked. "Would it be possible for you to give me a ride that far? That is to Los Angeles. I really need assistance and a ride to the next town would help a lot."

Phil looked at the man and not really

knowing what to say he asked the stranger. "If I give you a ride, do you intend to shoot me down the road a way once you got in my car?"

That seemed to stop the man short. It actually surprised Phil that he would say something like that to a total stranger.

Everything seemed to freeze at that moment. Phil was thinking to himself what he had said was just plain stupid and hurtful. The stranger was trying to figure out how he should react to the comment. They were both clearly caught off guard, Phil by the fact he had actually said that and the stranger by the fact that it was directed at him.

Stepping back the stranger raised both hands with palms facing Phil. "No sir, I would never do anything like that."

Again, they both stood there looking at one another. Actually, the situation was rather uncomfortable.

Finally, Phil smiled at the stranger and he started to laugh. The stranger's face was a little red and he was somewhat uneasy. "Yah got me."

Now they both were laughing and taking time for an awkward moment to pass by and fall dead on the parking lot before they continued.

They stood there talking for maybe five minutes when Phil finally told the stranger. "Yes, I will give you a ride, but you will have to pay for your own motel rooms and your share in the gas costs."

The stranger nodded and immediately reached into his pocket, pulled a wad of cash out, peeled a couple of hundred dollar bills off handing them to Phil. "I'll take care of my motel costs when we get there."

With that they shook hands and the stranger put his luggage in the trunk and they both got in the car and headed south toward California. From the rest stop to the greater Los Angeles area, it was about one thousand two hundred miles and that was running the distance on I-5. Phil planned on cutting over to the coast highway at Salem, Oregon and make the remainder of his run on the coast as he always did.

Phil then remembered. "Oh, by the way, what's your name?"

The stranger looked at him. "My name is Jewell Scarpone, but a lot of people call me Ruby. I got that name because I was born in July. But I would prefer to be called Jewell."

Jewell, thought Phil, that's an odd name

for a man. "Is that Juel like JUEL or what?"

Jewell knew that question was coming because is always did. "No, my name is actually Jewell spelled JEWELL. My mother gave it to me that way because, again, I was born in July.

Phil continued his interest in the stranger's name. "Scarpone, that sounds Italian to me, were your parents from Italy?"

"No, my great grandparents came from Sicily somewhere around the 1900's. They settled in the Chicago area and that is where my family had been all these years."

Phil nodded and offered his hand. "Well Jewell, my name is Phillip Morles, just call me Phil."

Phil started to think, *Sicily, that's where a lot of the mob type people came from. He lived in Chicago and I know that there are a lot of mob there also. Now, hold on, a name does not make a person part of the mob. He's probably perfectly all right, so put those thoughts away.*

Now most people would have never done what Phil just did. You are constantly warned by the authorities never to pick someone up that way, but for Phil this was not unusual. Phil's mom had continuously warned him about picking up strangers and that one day he would pay for it. Phil felt relatively sure Jewell was not a threat to him, but if he became a threat Phil would worry about it then.

On top of that Phil was curious about this guy. What was a person holding that much cash doing trying to find a ride at a rest stop in this part of the country? Curious, one would think he would be flying or at the least taking a bus, but no he was here at an I-5 rest stop in southwestern Washington, his curiosity was just too much.

Finally, after thinking how he would go about asking the question, Phil took the direct route. "Jewell, just how did you end up in that rest area anyway?"

Ah, the question. Jewell had been planning this part of the meeting for several days and he had his story well developed. On top of that, this guy asked the big question right on cue. So, Jewell started laying out his well-rehearsed reason for being there. "I had my own business in Kent, Washington and I lost everything due to the recession. I decided to go down around Los Angeles and the day before I was ready to leave, I had an accident and totaled my car.

19

"I was fortunate no one in either car was hurt. That really screwed up my plans. The last thing I wanted to do was go car shopping so I decided I would wait and buy a new car in Los Angeles.

"As it worked out a friend told me he was heading down the following week and said I could ride along. So, I closed all my legal matters out and packed what I wanted and headed south with my friend this morning. Just north of the rest area my friend got a call that his mother was seriously ill and he needed to return. So, he dropped me off here, at my request, and then headed back to Seattle. So here I am. That was two hours ago."

Jewell kept his eyes ahead and waited for Phil to respond as he was sure he would do in short order.

Phil thought what he had said was reasonable. After all a lot of businesses in that area were going under. "What was your business anyway?"

Continuing his story Jewell said. "I did importing of electronics from the orient. You know, computer parts, stereos, televisions, and so on. Had a fairly good business going and then it all fell apart. My problem was I had only been in it a short time and I was not able to hold on till things improved. It drove me into debt and so I cashed out and cleared out. I counted up my damages and ended up with a fairly good return on what I had left.

"I've got enough cash in the bank to start over. I felt that the southern California area would be a better place for me to start over. At least I hope so. Things don't look too good anywhere in the country and this is a hell of a poor time to try and start a new business.

"On top of that I'm single and have nothing to tie me to this area. My mother passed away about three years ago, so I really can go anywhere I wish. Southern California just looks like a great place to go. Whether I land in San Francisco or go on to L.A. doesn't matter. The fact of the matter is that L.A. is probably the better place."

Jewell then shifted the topic to Phil. "What do you do Phil?"

Phil looked over at Jewell and began. "Well, I'm involved in computer software. I work for a large software company in the northern Seattle area. No relationship with Microsoft. We troubleshoot beta software before it is released. I guess you could call me a computer geek or freak."

Waving his right hand, Jewell said. "Hey, there's nothing wrong with that. It just means you've got a load of brains and know how to use them. Is that a good paying job?

By this time Phil was becoming more relaxed and felt comfortable in their conversation. "Yeah, I guess you would say it was. Let me put it this way I have no money issues. And on top of that the future in my field is bright and growing."

Jewell then looked out the passenger window while asking. "Well, what are you going south for?"

Phil sighed and smiled at the thought of the warm southern California days. "Vacation, I have four weeks and I plan on taking a leisurely ride down the coast to Long Beach, relax for a few days and head back. I don't really care about the usual trappings for tourists. I have my own special places I like to stop and spend a day or a few hours. When I head home, I'll go through the wine country and load up on some of my favorites, go on home and back to work."

Jewell was thinking he had latched on to a good thing here. "Phil that is a great vacation, no schedules or place you have to be at any given time. Just go as you please and stop when you want."

Phil was starting to think about that very thing and then asked. "Jewell, I know that my stops could slow you down, so if you don't want to do all that, well it won't bother me if you decided to take another ride."

Jewell had halfway expected that reaction from Phil and now he had the opportunity to really link up with him. "No, no. Phil that sounds great. I was just hoping you would not alter it for my sake. No, if you want to stop some place, hey make me a part of it. This is great."

So, Jewell and Phil headed south. Phil knew enough about him to actually know nothing, but who gives a rip. People are different and he was and so Phil felt they could have a good time talking and seeing the many places he liked to stop. It felt good not to have to make this trip all by himself. Don't get him wrong, it would have made no difference if Jewell hadn't come along. Phil would still be making this trip and loving every second of it.

Phil had noticed Jewell had an accent and it sounded like it was from the Midwest or around there, it was definitely not from the

Pacific Northwest. No, he had heard that accent before and it fit in well with the Chicago area, in a lot of the gangster movies he had seen, the mob members sounded the same.

Yeah, he was originally from the Chicago area as he had said and not that long ago, but he had also said he had a business in the Seattle area and that could indicate he had been there for some time.

Priding himself on his ability to tie people to other areas of the states, Phil asked. "Hey, Jewell, you have a rather distinctive accent, how long has it been since you lived in the Chicago area?"

Jewell was a little bit surprised by the accuracy of Phil's comment. "Yeah, I lived there most of my life until my mom decided she wanted to move to Seattle, so I came with her. That was just after I had graduated from school and I had little if any idea as to what I wanted to do. It seems like it was so long ago. Anyway, once a Chicagoan you're always a Chicagoan."

As he talked, he was looking around all the time. Phil could see this guy missed nothing. His eyes were constantly moving. They were blue, but had a dark hue to them, piercing and hard. Phil found himself watching him. If he didn't know better, he would think Jewell was expecting something. Just what it was, he had no idea, but something was digging him. Yeah, he could tell, something was digging deep down inside and it was not letting him relax.

How much more should he ask Jewell about his past? That was becoming a serious issue for Phil. He could see this guy had a background and that made him much more curious about Jewell and his past, but there was a point when too much digging could get him into trouble, and besides that, it was not polite.

Phil was planning on cutting over to Highway 101 at Salem, Oregon and then making his run south on the coast highway. This was his favorite part of his trip south and back north when he came home. There were dozens of locations along the route he liked and planned to stop at. His main aim was several art galleries along the Oregon coast and then on the California coast in the area of Carmel.

The entire area from Carmel to Santa Barbara was loaded with local crafts shops. He loved that type of ware and had a large collection of this kind of art work. Many of the store owners knew him by sight and name and almost always had something there they felt would interest him. There were few stops between here and the Cabrillo Highway or State Route 1. Once on the Cabrillo he would be stopping almost continually and he didn't know if Jewell would be too pleased.

Phil continued to advise Jewell of his plans and that he could bail any time he wanted. "Well Jewell, anytime you feel that I'm going to slow for you I'll gladly take you to a bus stop or whatever and let you off, How's that?"

Jewell was not too sure this guy really wanted him along with all the offers to drop him off or not being offended if he decided to leave. "Great Phil, but I can assure you that you have spiked my interest and I will probably stay the course."

Phil was starting to get irritating, but continued to make his point. "You're sure now?"

For a second Jewell wanted to reach over and grab him by the throat and shake him while saying. "Yeah, it sounds great."

All Phil had to do was lay it down and leave it behind, but he had to say one last thing. "All right, but remember, once were on the Cabrillo there are few ways away from it. You generally have to go all the way or turn around and head back north."

Jewell remained patient and went along with the talk. "No, Phil, that's all right with me."

Jewell took a shot at changing the subject. "By the way Phil, you told me what you did and where, but where, do you come from or live?"

Phil jumped at the opportunity. "Well, we." He paused. "I lived in the town of Everett, Washington. That's just a few miles north of Seattle. I was born in that area and just never found any reason to leave. I received all my training and education from the local schools and then I attended the University of Washington, majoring in Computer Science."

Jewell caught the little change in Phil's voice. "You started to say we and then changed. Are you married or something?"

That brought back old wounds and Phil said. "Jewell I was, but that didn't work out. I still slip and refer to us instead of me. It's only been ten months and I'm still adjusting. It was not a great part of my life and I've had to rebuild everything and get my mind straight."

Jewell realized this guy had some issues that maybe he didn't want to get involved in. "Hey man, I'm sorry about that. Hope I didn't open up any old wounds. I can't relate to your situation in that I have never been married. Guess I just couldn't find a woman who would put up with me and my ways."

Phil was thinking and wishing he had not brought that out of him. "No, it's all right, just an adjustment thing and nothing else. I've been able to put that under the bridge and move on. Just from time to time, it manages to slip back in to my mind."

By this time, they had reached Portland, about forty-five miles south from where Phil picked Jewell up and Phil decided to stop and get something to eat.

Portland had been the place where Phil had first met his ex-wife. He had gone there for a software seminar at the Hilton Hotel downtown and she was one of the presenters. They hit it off right away. It was one of those whirlwind affairs and they were married within a year.

They managed to make it two years before the polish wore off and they lost touch with one another. Who's fault? Guess it was a joint thing, but Phil was most of the problem. He was not made to be married at the time and it showed. With his career issues and his desire to take long trips on his own, it was not what he or she had expected.

They were fortunate to not have had any children. It had not been a hard divorce, when you consider some of the nightmares you see around the country, but it still had not been smooth and easy. It wasn't the sharing or dividing of their possessions, it had been the fact that he had failed her and had wanted to live his old lifestyle along with the new one. No, she had tried, but he had not and the end result was inevitable.

Yes, Portland was a place that held a lot of good memories, but that's old history and not his life now. It's a nice city of around four hundred thousand, sitting on the Willamette River on the south side of the Washington and Oregon Border and the Columbia River. I guess you would call Portland a rather liberal city, much like Seattle.

He quickly shoved that back in his mind and asked. "Jewell, you ever spend time in Portland?"

In reality Jewell knew little or nothing

about this part of the country. He had never spent any time on the west coast and said. "No, I've never been here before."

His demeanor seemed to change a little as they came into the main part of the city. Phil had taken the Interstate 205 bypass of the main downtown area of the city, but still they were in a heavily populated area.

A large city could be a problem for someone in the situation Jewell was in. He knew he had to keep alert in large metropolitan areas. "From the looks of it I probably would not like this place that much. We're stopping here?" Jewell asked.

"Thought we would for lunch, is that all right?" Phil looked over at Jewell. "There are several good places along here and frankly I'm getting hungry." Phil continued.

About then Jewell realized he was hungry as well. "Yeah, I'm feeling like I could eat."

Phil was familiar with the Interstate 205 area and had always used it, that way he could skirt the main part of the city on the east side. Just then Phil pulled off onto a service exit and continued on about half a mile to an Outback Restaurant he had been to before.

Jewell was getting more and more

uneasy as they pulled into the parking lot. He would not have parked where Phil had selected, but then Phil was not as careful as Jewell was. They got out of the car and started walking toward the restaurant, all the while Jewell's eyes were looking the area over and over.

Phil had noticed Jewell's actions and it gave Phil the impression he was worried about something or someone. He thought it better not to ask at that time, but there was something going on and he may want to know what it was before too long.

As they entered the restaurant Jewell moved toward the back of the main dining area and took a seat in the far corner so he was facing out toward the rest of the dining area. He selected a seat that he could see the front door from and also gave him a clear unobstructed view of everyone there. They settled in and had a good meal. After an hour they paid up and headed out.

They were there maybe an hour and fifteen minutes and then back on the road heading south for Salem. As they merged back onto Interstate 205 Jewell seemed to relax a little bit. And Phil simply let the issue settle back in his mind and left it there.

They were on their way to Salem, which is the capital of Oregon State and is about an hour's drive south of the greater Portland area. As they approached the area, Phil was watching for the turn off to get onto the Salem Parkway old Highway 99E. They followed that to the Dallas Salem Highway 22 which took them west toward the coast. They continued on to the Wilamina Salem highway 22 and continued on toward the coast where they tied into Coastal Highway 101 at the Hebo Junction and then turned south toward Lincoln City, a total of around one hundred miles.

All this time they carried on a small talk type conversation in relationship to the area they were driving through. Phil could tell this was the first time for Jewell in this part of the country and he was engrossed in everything they saw. He was especially interested in the Elk and Deer they saw as they headed toward the coast.

"I've never seen country like this before." Jewell said. "That area up around the rest stop where we met at was much like this, but not as mountainous. The area around Seattle is different as well I guess it's all the people and traffic. I like this part of the country, could settle down here in a heartbeat."

"Why don't you?" Phil asked.

Jewell was relaxing now and starting to loosen up a little more. "Well, in about six months I would start to become nervous and wanting to get back to the larger population areas. That's all I know and it's probably where I should stay."

As they pulled onto Highway 101 and spotted the ocean for the first time Jewell became glued to the passenger door window. It was a total change in his demeanor and attention.

Jewell couldn't help it. What he was seeing he had never expected. "I have never seen anything like this before. At first it looked like the great lakes, but just the sight of it speaks size and power. No, it communicated that it was the master of the world's waterways and it carried power behind it."

Phil caught that immediately and it disturbed him because of the intensity of Jewell's reaction to seeing the Pacific. He said he had never seen that before. Odd, he has lived in Seattle a number of years and he has never seen the Pacific. Phil had never met anyone who lived in the Seattle area for any period of time that had not gone to and seen the Pacific.

That is really odd. Phil's spine seemed to prickle when he thought of it. No one who has lived in the Seattle area for any period of time has not been to or seen the Pacific Ocean at least once. He decided to keep his thoughts to himself, but all the warning flags were up and waving at gale force.

Jewell was really getting excited. Like a child who saw its first toy or pet or whatever. It made no sense and that caused Phil to start to second think taking Jewell on. All of Jewell's attention was riveted on the view in front of him. "The waves, I've got to get down there and see them up close. Can we find a place where we can stop? I really need to go out there and see them close up."

Phil had not expected this kind of a reaction. He was almost certain that Jewell would jump from the car to get down to the beach. He then said "Jewell I think there is a parking area just up the road. We'll pull in there and you can get an up-close look at the waves."

Jewell waved his left hand at Phil as he kept looking out the passenger door window at the specter in front of him. Just what was in this man that would make him react like that, like a man living his last days, a man short on time with much to do and much to see.

Phil finally found a parking spot just south of Neskowin and pulled over. Jewell was out of the car almost before it came to a stop. He literally ran down the path to the beach and then across the beach to the water. He stopped short of running into the waves and just stood there.

Phil was caught completely unprepared for Jewell's action. When he caught up to him, he looked at Phil. The look in his eyes told a story, one that brought Phil to the point of deep concern. This guy was completely out of his realm. He had no idea as to what he was doing or where he was at. All he could see were the waves coming in on that conveyer belt of nature.

It was like looking at a child seeing its first Christmas tree. The look in his eyes was one of surprise and excitement but his overall demeanor was clearly of someone who was confused. Not really knowing what this was all about or just how he should act.

Jewell's whole body was in a state of hyper activity. "Listen to that." He would say.

"Can you hear that? That is the most powerful force I have ever heard or seen in my life. Even the Atlantic can't match that force and power."

Phil was still trying to regain his own equilibrium. *What? What the hell was he talking about anyway? What is going on here with this guy?* Phil was certain Jewell was not under the influence of any drugs. He had been completely rational before they came into view of the Pacific. He had never seen anyone react to something this way before.

Jewell was leaning and turning the side of his head to the ocean. "That sound the waves make. It's like the pounding of your heart. It's a beat that come from the deepest parts of the world and it is nonstop and forever. It's ageless and of such force that it makes me feel insignificant."

Phil went from trying to catch up to a state of bewilderment. "All right, so what?"

Jewell was almost frantic in his action. "Can't you hear it? Can't you see the force and power that is behind those waves? It literally screams power, an unstoppable force that no man or nation can stand against."

Phil was trying to understand. "Hear what Jewell, what are you talking about?"

To a person who has heard these waves their entire life there was nothing special to what they were hearing. It was the beach, the ocean and that was the way it sounded all the time. What's the big deal anyway?

Jewell stopped and took a deep breath and then looked at Phil, "It's the power, that never ending power that they have. It has force behind it, so much force it hurts the ears. I have never seen or heard anything like it." Jewell stood there looking at Phil with this almost crazy look in his eyes. It was not a threatening look it was more a look of loneliness, of insignificance, a look that told Phil this man was hiding something and that something was monumental.

Phil stood still a few minutes and listened. To him it was the sound of the waves breaking and rolling onto the beach, a comforting sound. He could not relate to what Jewell was talking about. The ocean did not present that magnitude of an issue to Phil. He guessed maybe he was too used to it or something. He had always found comfort in the sound of the waves as they came ashore. When you stood there and looked out at the surf you could see a region out away from the beach where there was a mass of waves piling up one behind the other. From that area there was a continual roar of power.

As each wave separated itself from the mass of power, they would quietly cruise onto the beach and lap at your feet. They came from a raging mass of water breaking one over the other and out of that achieved symmetry and shape that carried it all the way to its final end.

Phil looked at Jewell and shrugged his shoulders. "No, they sound normal to me."

Jewell wasn't going to let it alone, to him it was power and, in that power, he found a comfort that few others ever achieve in the surf. He then said. "That's because you're used to them. To me they speak of vast amounts of time and energy being pushed ashore by its power. How much time has passed while those waves have washed against this beach? It's been millions of years and it has millions to go. They have witnessed the push of mankind through history, all the heartache and death that has accompanied mankind in his search for the control of all things of this world."

By this time Phil was thinking that Jewell was a nut case, a right out of the trees' nut case.

Jewell was calming down now and relaxing. "I know, that sounds odd to you, but, to me this is absolutely the most unbelievable thing I have ever experienced. Look at that. The great lakes never gave me that feeling. God, I could spend a life time here, just watching and listening to it. I could sit down right here and stay for a hundred years and let it speak to me and tell me all the things it has seen and experienced."

They spent maybe an hour standing there looking out across the water. It was a good thing in that Jewell was able to calm down and gain a degree of calmness and rest for his soul. A moment in time where his past could wait and the future had not been invented yet and the present could simply exist. Phil was able to observe and gain a little more understanding of this stranger he had given a ride to.

In the back of Phil's mind, he was beginning to build a relationship with this person. He found he was beginning to read him and knew that here was a man with some rather large issues working their ways through his mind. He had a burden he was carrying and that burden, in time, would make itself known. Phil was not sure if he wanted to know it or not, well not at this time anyway.

As they turned and walked back to the car Jewell asked. "Is that the same ocean we will be seeing all the way to California?" He was looking back at the surf and trying to walk a straight line back to the car. It was a near impossible task to say the least.

Phil was a little set back by his question. Didn't this guy go to school or something? "Yeah, it is. That's the Pacific it's the biggest of them all." Phil replied.

As they approached the car and road, Jewell's demeanor shifted back to that careful and watchful being Phil had become accustomed to in the short time he had known Jewell.

Jewell nodded and looked back. "Who would have thought?" There was a change to his demeanor, a sense of dreaminess, like he could simply sit down on the ground right there and remain for the rest of his life.

They continued on into Lincoln City and found Phil's favorite motel. It sits right on the beach and had plenty of openings. Jewell made sure he got one on the ocean side and ground floor. He wanted to be able to go out the door and walk out onto the beach at any time. Phil told him it cost considerably more for a ground floor, ocean front room.

Jewell just shrugged. "Some things are worth the extra cost." It was clear that his experience with the Pacific was not over yet and may not be for some time.

Phil got a room on the second floor and just happened to end up over Jewell's room. During the course of the night, he heard the sliding door to Jewell's room open and close at least a half dozen times. What the hell was he doing? When he got up and looked out his window, he could see nothing. There was a full moon that night and he could see no one moving around on the beach.

That morning when he finally got up and looked out the window, Jewell was standing about ninety feet from the door to his room facing the ocean, just looking. There was something going on here and Phil was not sure he wanted to know anything about it, but on the other hand he was curious as to what was going on.

As he was watching, Jewell turned and started walking back to his room. He looked up and saw Phil and he waved at Jewell. Jewell just looked down and walked on in to his room. Maybe thirty seconds later Phil's phone rang. It was Jewell and he sounded a little eager. "Are you ready for breakfast?"

Phil started to ask and then said. "Yeah, I am."

"Me too, meet you at the car." Jewell replied.

Strange Phil thought, he then got cleaned up and ready and then went and checked out and walked out to the car. Jewell was sitting on the front fender looking out across the beach at the ocean.

Phil was coming to understand that this guy was a person used to ordering others around. He was independent and usually got his own way. There was a force behind the demeanor of this man and it was one that Phil would come to know well.

"You ready for breakfast?" Phil asked.

Jewell looked at him and then back to the ocean. "Yeah, I could eat a dozen eggs right now."

They walked across the street to a small restaurant sitting back from the road, one of those ma and pa type places. As they entered the place Jewell headed for the rear of the main dining area and took a table moving to the far side with his back to the wall. The waitress brought them menus and they ordered coffee. When she brought the coffee, they were ready to order. Jewell stayed away from a dozen eggs, but did have a steak and egg dish along with all the trimmings. Phil settled for a stack of pancakes and bacon strips.

As they ate Phil noted that Jewell literally attacked his meal. He was one of those eating is for eating and not conversation type persons and he went at his food with gusto. He had noticed that at the Outback restaurant the day before as well.

Phil wanted to ask Jewell about his reactions to the Pacific but decided not to go that route at that time. He knew he would need to in time, but felt the right time was not now and it would become evident when that time came up. Yet, he still had that need to know bugging him. It would have to be sooner than later.

They got back to the car and were ready to pull out when Phil turned to Jewell. He just had to ask, there was no way around it. It was not going to be later it was going to be now. He had to know. "Jewell, is there anything wrong?"

Jewell looked at Phil and then turned his head and looked out the window. "What do you mean?"

Phil felt he had to pursue this issue right then and there. He could feel that there was something and it was not just a small issue. It could well involve him somewhere along the way. "You seem to be bothered by something and I just thought it may help to talk it out."

Jewell seemed to want to talk, but then said. "No, it's just the ocean. I've never seen anything just like it and it seemed to have made an odd impression on me, know what I mean. It makes me feel so small and vulnerable. It makes me wonder if all I have done in my life was worth all the effort and pain.

He paused and sat there as they pulled out onto the 101 and headed south out of town. "I'm all right, just a little nostalgia thing. I'll get over it. All right, where we off to today? "

Phil decided to let it lay for the time being. "We're going on south and seeing what there is to see as we go. There's just a thousand miles of coastline between here and L.A. And, by the way, if you see anything you would like to stop for just ask me and we'll stop. I love that kind of out of the box, spur of the moment thing."

Jewell looked at him and smiled. "Sounds great to me, man I'm going to love this trip."

Phil turned his attention to his driving and headed south out of Lincoln City and on to the next stop down the road. The weather was perfect for this time of year in this area of Oregon. It was almost the perfect situation. He was into his second day of his vacation and had nothing to do but his annual trip down the coast and through all the towns and scenic areas he had become accustomed to. Perfect, just perfect and he was going to take advantage of it. Right now, he felt that nothing could ever change this part of his trip, absolutely nothing.

The only difference was the guy in the passenger seat. Had he made an error in agreeing to take Jewell along with him? So far everything was going fine and he could see no reason to believe it would not continue and eventually end that way once they reached L.A. Perfect, yeah everything was just perfect and he had nothing to worry about, nothing at all.

Chapter Two

THE FIND

It was about nine o'clock in the morning and Norman Howard was just entering his second area of timber stands. It was his job to cruise the timber sections assigned to him that week and select and mark trees for harvest. He usually carried out these surveys about three to four months before the actual harvest. He had been doing this work for some eight years and was the company's chief timber cruiser. Each section was surveyed and then classified as to its production capacity. There was a projected production target of so many board feet of lumber and it was his task to determine which trees would be cut to meet that production target.

He had just turned onto a log road on the east side of Interstate 5 maybe a mile to a mile and a half, as the crow flies, from the east side Toutle River Rest area on Interstate 5. The road itself was about half a mile south of the Old Jackson Highway overpass at mile post 57 just off of the Hill Creek Road. The overpass road was the Roger's Road and it tied into the Old Jackson South Highway. This particular road was just south of the Lewis and Cowlitz County line. The line was actually just across a ravine from the road he was on.

He advised dispatch of his location "Dispatch, Howard."

"Go ahead Howard." The dispatcher replied.

"Dispatch I am in the north sector Cowlitz County and will be south to 504."

"Received Howard."

The weather was perfect for that time of year and he would find the task enjoyable and relaxing. At that time of the morning the air was still sharp with the smell of the morning floating over hills and ridges. It was one of those times when one felt at peace with one's self.

This particular road would intersect with State Route 504 to the south, so he had to start surveying as soon as he got on to company land. This was his third stop and he could see at least five good trees off to his right and up the hill. In this particular section he was not looking at a clear-cut project, this was to be a selective cut for thinning this section.

His job was to measure and then determining the board feet production for the tree or trees in a selected stand. He was working to achieve a certain amount of board feet from each individual section. This process required that he measure the selected trees in a stand.

He parked his truck on the road just down from the first tree he was targeting. He collected his tape and scope and notebook and started up the side of the ridge. As he approached the first of the five trees, he took his measuring tape and started to take the circumference measurement of the tree. He had made it about three quarters of the way around the tree when he stepped on something slippery and almost fell. As he looked down to where he had stepped, he saw an off-white dome or bowl buried in the ground about half way.

That's strange, who would bury a bowl around here. There were no berries to pick here and it did not appear that there had been any camping around the area. Then on the other hand this could have been here for many years and just now was unearthed.

As he leaned over to get a better look at the object it made him catch his breath. It wasn't a bowl, it was bone. It appeared to be the top of a human head. He moved around to get a better look at the thing and was sure that it was a human head without the flesh or hair attached.

He pulled his tape off the tree and backed down and away from the tree and its hidden secret. When he got to his truck, he called dispatch. "Dispatch Howard."

"Go ahead Howard."

"Dispatch I think I just found a body. All I could see was the top of the head. Would you call the Sheriff's Office advise them of my find and to send someone out here to check this out."

Forty minutes later a deputy pulled up behind his truck. As the deputy approached, the lumberman walked to meet him and they met at the back of his pickup. He explained to the deputy just what he was doing in the area and what he had found just up the hill from where they were standing.

The lumberman and deputy walked up to the tree and the top of the head was pointed out to the deputy. After a few minutes of pulling the leaves and dirt away from the top of the head, he confirmed that it was a person buried there. With that the deputy took the company man back to their vehicles and reported in to the sheriff's dispatch. "152 County."

"Go ahead 152."

"County I have confirmed a body at the location. Request you advise the office and dispatch an investigative unit out to this location."

"Received 152. They have been advised and are in route."

"152"

Meanwhile the deputy took a roll of barrier tape back to the tree and cordoned off the area around the tree. You've seen it before. It's a yellow tape with the words "Police or Sheriff Line- Do Not Cross". The deputy cordoned off an area about seventy-five-by-seventy-five feet. Then he took his notebook and started writing down everything on the company and what the employee was doing in the area.

After about twenty minutes he finished with the preliminary interview and told the employee to sit in his truck until the investigators arrived. If they had nothing else for him, then he would be free to go.

Over the course of the next seven hours the side of the hill was crawling with police personnel. Finally, the coroner was called in and the body excavated and removed. A search of the victim determined he was still in a pair of lounging pajamas and had a number of gunshot wounds on his body and to the middle of his forehead. They determined that there were no identification documents on the body.

Once that was done and the body had been removed by the coroner the investigators then laid out a search grid of the area and they brought in extra personnel to do a walking search of the hill side for a half mile in both directions along the road and up to the top of ridge.

As with any search the amounts and types of junk and waste found along any road anywhere was significant. For the most part they were drink cans and car parts. But, up on the hillside one item would prove to be the most significant and would break this mystery wide open.

One of the searchers was finishing up a line sweep and was working himself down the hill when he thought he saw something odd about ten yards to his left. As he moved over in that direction, he found a forty-gallon green plastic garbage can. The can had a large amount of duct tape all over the outside up by where the lid would have been. He called out that he found something and investigators started up the hill.

As they approached the find one of them saw the lid for a garbage can lying in the brush, it too had a lot of duct tape on it, and he marked it.

Both the can and lid were recovered marked and taken as evidence. There was still the slight smell of decomposition left in the can and on the lid. After the rest of the search was completed all found items, which included a new shovel found just another hundred feet from where the garbage can was found. These were then taken to the Sheriff's Office and the team started to go through them. Naturally the can and lid were the primary area of concern.

Over at the coroners they had determined that the subject had been shot multiple times. It looked like he had been sprayed with bullets leaving little doubt as to how he was killed. He had round hits in his arms, hands, legs, neck, upper torso, lower torso and one right through the forehead. There was no doubt that someone wanted him dead.

There were no identification papers on the body or any telltale marks or tattoos that could be used to help identify him. Finger prints were taken and a search of state and national files was initiated. At that point there were no means to determine who or where he came from.

Back at the Sheriff's Office they had gotten around to checking the garbage can out and while looking it over one of the detectives spotted a piece of paper on the bottom of the can. It's strange how some things turn out. Here was this small piece of paper that had been attached to the bottom of the can with a piece of packaging tape and somehow it had managed to stay there.

When they retrieved it, they found that it was a sales receipt for the can with a listed price of $27.47. However, the most important thing was the name of the store and the address where the can was purchased.

Bickles Hardware, in Tinley Park, Illinois, it was apparent that it was not one of the large chain stores around the country. No, this one had to be a local store that would be found in just one place, Tinley Park, Illinois That turned out to be a suburb of Chicago, Illinois. A check of the map found the town just south of Chicago, just northwest of the junction of Interstates 57 and 80.

A call back to the Tinley Park Police resulted in information that they had a missing person from that town and they had classified it as a probable homicide. The information concerning the missing person stated he had been reported missing by his father and when the police went to the scene, they found a crime scene almost beyond belief.

Literally there had been a gun fight, no a gun battle had taken place in the bedroom of the missing person's home. The place had been completely shot up. There wasn't a wall or spot on the ceiling that did not have a bullet hole in it.

It appeared someone had been in the

bed when the battle started because of the amount of blood and the number of bullet holes, spent casings and several guns around and on the bed. The fact was there was blood everywhere in the place. As best as they could tell at this time the blood was from just one individual and DNA testing had shown the blood to be that of their missing person.

Just by the magnitude of the number of rounds that had been shot and the fact that only two types of cartridges where present, the surviving party could have a reasonable ground of self-defense. Yes, it was the victim's home, but by the looks of things there had been no forced entry and there had been a number of rounds that hit the edge of the bedroom door and then ran along the wall from the door to the right about chest high. One officer stated that it looked like an ambush.

They, the Washington authorities that is, were fairly sure that they had the body of the missing person right there in the coroner's office in Cowlitz County, Washington. That fact alone stunned everyone.

With that information the investigators in both Washington and Illinois had determined that after the gun battle the living individual took the body and transported it the one thousand seven hundred sixty-four plus miles from Tinley Park to the grave site in Cowlitz County. It was unreal. It was almost unbelievable, yet the facts showed that it was true.

The question now was, who was the individual that killed the victim and then transported him all that distance to bury him, and, on top of that why? Why would he take the body and haul it that distance just to bury it? There had to be a significant reason for the person to go to such lengths.

The number of places between Washington and Illinois where he could have disposed of the body simply made the whole situation totally weird. In time they would discover the whole true story, but right now it was a matter of disbelief.

After further exchanges of information and checks of fingerprints they determined that the name of the individual who was found in the grave in Washington was Benjamin Cipozzio. While talking with officers in Tinley Park it was learned that the Cipozzio family was fairly well known in organized crime circles in the greater Chicago area. When they notified the family that they had found their missing son they had a distinct feeling that it would not be just the police who would be looking for the killer.

Any attempt to gain helpful information from the family failed. Word on the street was that there was a friend of the dead man missing as well and the family was considering that individual as the killer. If he was not, then they were sure he knew who the killer was and that he would either help them, when they found him, or he would wish he had.

On the other hand, it could be that this subject, like his friend was missing as well. A check of his home found that he had not been there for at least three weeks. There were no indications of any foul play at his residence. It appeared he had packed and left. A number of weapons were found in the residence and indications that there had been others simply by the fact that he had ammunition there for weapons that were not present. His name was Jewell Scarpone. A nationwide search for Mister Scarpone was put into effect. All they could do was sit and wait for some results to develop.

Following up the information that had been learned so far, an attempt was made to try and determine the route that had been taken to bring the body to Washington State. Between the two police agencies they agreed to take the stand that only one of the two men was in fact dead and the other had been the one to transport the body and that person was probably the killer.

The first task was trying to determine the main route the killer would have taken when he left the Chicago area. They set up a team to try and trace his path across the country. They had three main Interstate routes, I-80, I-90, and I-94. It was decided to follow the I-90 to try to determine where the subject may have stayed while heading west.

The second team concentrated on trying to trace the subject's activities through his credit cards, if he had any. It was hoped that both would come together and give the agencies a clear route he had taken as he traveled across country.

At this point they had the probable name of the killer and the name of the victim. They knew where the crime had taken place and knew that the victim had been buried in Washington State. That meant the body had been transported over one thousand seven hundred miles from the place where the victim was killed to the place where he was disposed of. They also knew that the victim was related to the head of a mob family in the greater Chicago area and they were probably hunting this Mister Scarpone as well. They knew they were in a race.

Further checks by the Tinley Park Police found a vehicle owned by Mister Scarpone was missing. It was a 2003 Buick LaCrosse with Illinois plates. An all-points bulletin was issued for that vehicle and the owner. The dragnet had been started. The problem was they had no idea how much of a head start the suspect had. The battle had taken place three to four weeks earlier which meant that they were behind the action by at least a month to a month and a half.

In addition, the police knew the family was working this case as well and they had no idea as to how much of a head start the Cipozzio family had on them. They knew that Ben, that is Benjamin Cipozzio, had been killed and his body had been removed and later found in Washington State. They were in a race against time and if they did not find Mr. Scarpone first, they would probably never find him. It was not a good picture and it was going to get much worse before it started to get better.

Chapter Three

THE KILLING

The damn phone rang at six thirty and pulled Jewell from a deep sleep. He had only gotten to bed around three o'clock and was in need of a good eight hours. He managed to drag himself up out of his sleep and answer the phone. It was Ben, Benjamin Cipozzio.

Jewell wanted to hang up but thought better of it. "Ben, what the hell do you want this time of the morning?"

Ben was one of those guys that did as he pleased and people usually responded in the positive to his calling on them. This time it was business and he was not going to accept any crap from anyone. "Jewell, I told you last week that you had to make good on that job by this morning, have you done it yet?"

Jewell instantly went mad. "Look Ben,

I told you I would try, not that I would do it. What's with you anyway? You've never been this demanding in the past and frankly you're pissing me off."

After a few seconds pause Ben continued. "Look Jewell, it's just that I'm in a pinch and I need that job done."

By now Jewell was fully awake and thinking at flank speed. "Ben, you never told me it was something urgent. You just asked me to do it. You know that I'm not into those things and I told you that I may do it. I did not tell you I would."

After just a few seconds Ben was off the chart angry and he let Jewell know it. "Jewell, don't screw me on this. If you weren't going to do it for me then you should have said it right out."

Jewell could tell he was building up a real fit by the tone of his voice. "Yeah, and then I have to live with your never-ending bitching about it. Ben, I'm going to hang up now and go back to sleep. Don't call me back. When I get up, I'll call you and we'll get this thing you want done worked out."

Ben was yelling and shaking the phone. "Don't do this to me Jewell."

Jewell interrupted Ben. "Ben, enough

of this, I'll call you later."

It was no big deal. At least Jewell didn't think so. He couldn't figure out why Ben was so insistent on him doing that stupid little job for him. He's not a strong arm, but he had done jobs in the past and didn't like them. Now Ben wants him to go and punch out some little shop keeper for not increasing his payments to Ben and his family. Hell, there are dozens of guys out there who would love to do that job, why did it have to be him?

Six hours later Jewell got up and showered and shaved and had a light lunch. He then picked up the phone and called Ben.

Jewell expected a hard time with Ben. "Yeah, Ben Jewell here."

Jewell was right and Ben came off at him, "What the hell you calling for?"

Jewell patiently told Ben that he was calling back as he said he would six hours ago. "Ben, I told you that after I got some sleep, I would call you and we would work this thing out.

Ben's voice went dry and threatening. "To late Jewell, I had Sammy do the job."

Jewell's attention was heightened by this time. "Good then I don't have to worry about it."

Ben wouldn't let it lay. "Yeah, you do Jewell. We've been friends for a long time, but when I ask you to do something for me you don't have the option of telling me you might."

Jewell was fully up and ready for Ben's attitude and came back. "Hold on Ben, I'm not one of your soldiers. I'm not even a part of your organization. You said it, we have been friends for years, but that does not make me a part of your organization or family, understand?"

Ben pushed the point and pressed his position. "Jewell, you've benefited from our relationship and from my perspective that makes you mine."

Jewell had had it by this time and let Ben have it. "Screw you Ben, I'm nobodies and that's it.

Ben had now become menacing. "Don't make me have to send someone to talk to you Jewell.

Jewell was now building a real anger base himself. "Ben, you pull that stupid shit with me and I'll cut your heart out.

Jewell continued. "Now, are we going to work this out or am I going to have to end this friendship and move on."

Ben pushed his point. "Jewell, you're too deep into our partnership."

Jewell responded. "Oh, now it's a partnership. When you want something like a little old man beat up, I'm your subordinate. When you want to talk about our business relationship, we're now partners. Yes, Ben I want to keep the partnership going, but not at the expense of my own freedom, understand."

Ben became more agreeable by this time. "Come on Jewell, relax. Leave the other thing behind and let's get busy with our project. How about you coming over this afternoon and we'll work out the rest of the issues on that job we have coming up."

Jewell knew when one of these guys changed their attitude that way, it was not over. It was just getting started. "All right Ben, I'll be over in about an hour."

By this time Ben was quiet and responded. "See you then Jewell."

Jewell was now fishing. "Ben?"

"Yeah, Jewell."

Jewell calmly asked. "We're really straight on that issue."

Ben said with a flat voice. "Yeah, you were right, I over stepped my bounds."

Ben hung up and Jewell sat there. No, it

was not all right. He could tell Ben was stewing and it was not all right. In the next two hours Jewell would either be dead or well on his way to making a fortune.

Jewell had learned over the years while associating with those in the rackets you had to stay on your toes. You had to be watching all the time. One small word or slip and those people would kill you.

He had known Ben for around twenty years, since high school. They hit it off well. Jewell had known Ben's family background all along and never let that bother him. Ben's dad was the head of a family in the greater Chicago area and by family he didn't mean moms and dads and kids. He was talking about the mob, you know La Cosa Nostra, the Mafia. That didn't bother Jewell, he liked Ben and that was all that was important.

Jewell had decided to venture out on a different but related career. He had decided he wanted to be something or someone special, someone with special abilities that were in demand and were not too common. An occupation that when needed paid big money.

I guess you would call him special. He had spent years honing his skills. He knew his trade better than most and his varied tools were extensive. His services were not always in demand, but when they were, he could name his price.

There are many names for his career path such as Contractor, Mechanic, Shooter, Trigger-man, Assassin, Cleaner, Iceman, Hit man. Yes, he was a loner, a contract killer who was well known within the world of the mob. He carried a special identification, but we won't go into that right now. All that is important here is that he was familiar with death and the process of applying it in a skilled and direct manner.

Being a freelancer, he had no allegiance to any family or mob boss. He kept it that way, remaining neutral in everything. When called, he would accept the proposed offer, if the price was right. It made no difference if he knew the target or not. Once the contract was given, he would and did fulfill it. Who knows how many contracts he has fulfilled over the years?

Anyway, Ben's dad was a cool guy and let them hang together and generally covered all the expenses during their fun years. Once they finished school Ben started working for his father and offered to include Jewell. Jewell told Ben he wanted to stay friends with

Ben, but was not interested in being a part of his father's business.

In his neighborhood, that was not the norm. Other young men dreamed of being in the rackets and living high and wild. What most did not know was that just a few had the mettle and smarts to reach that level of success. The majority spent their life being told what to do, when to do it, how to do it and they paid dearly if they failed. The soldier's life was at the bottom of the food chain and they either died or went to prison for the rest of their lives.

Jewell picked a different direction and it was one he had the talent and ability to do and do well. When he was present everyone knew who he was and wondered if he was there on business. They just never knew and that is what scared them the most about this man.

Ben accepted Jewell's desire to not become just one of the gangs and they continued their friendship. Over the years Jewell had done a number of favors for Ben, some of which were clearly against the law, but that's what a friend is for.

In time Ben approached Jewell about a deal he thought the two of them could do and make a bunch of money. "What is that, Ben?"

"Drugs Jewell, Drugs."

"I don't know Ben, that's a high-risk area."

"Yeah, but if we hit it big, we're rich beyond our wildest dreams." Ben replied.

Jewell had thought it over for a couple of weeks and finally went to Ben's home and told him he would play along. That is how they got into the drug trafficking partnership. For the next five months they worked setting things up.

Jewell demanded that they keep the activity restricted to as few people as possible, and he wanted to check out each new entry into the deal himself to ensure that they weren't cops. Ben agreed and they went to work.

Time and again Ben asked Jewell if he wanted to be part of the family and time and again Jewell would tell him no. "Ben I want to stay free and loose. I don't want to join up with anyone. I want to remain my own boss and not under someone else. Thanks for the offer, but no thanks."

Each time Ben seemed to be a little irritated, but would acknowledge Jewell's refusal and continue on with whatever they were doing.

Jewell made good money freelancing in selling car electronics, or just about anything else he could carry in his car or store in his home. The cops would call him a fence, but from his perspective he was just a business man buying supplies on an open market. How was he to know that any particular item was stolen or not. He was not a pawn shop owner. He bought outright and sold at a profit. You know the American dream.

It didn't hurt that he knew people in powerful places such as Ben's dad and Ben for that matter. The ability to drop a name or two almost always got him favors with those he was dealing with. Especially those who were bringing not quite legal products to him. I guess it was only normal for Ben and his dad to expect something for his use of their names, but so far that had not become a major issue. He was sure it was about to become just that in just a couple of hours.

As he prepared to head over to Ben's he had this nagging feeling that things were not quite right. Ben had become too cooperative all of a sudden and that can often mean trouble in capital letters. He went to his closet and took out two Glock Model 22 40 caliber semi-automatic guns. He also pulled out four clips, each one loaded with fifteen .40 caliber rounds. He decided he was going over armed for war, just in case. Past experience had taught him that you never take chances with those in the Mafia.

As he left his house his mind was spinning with possibilities and how he would react to them. Over the years Jewell had learned to become exceptionally proficient in the use of weapons, just about any type of weapon that came along. He was a natural planner and knew he would need to watch for any of Ben's associates in or around the house. If he saw any, then he was sure that this meeting had one and only one ending to it, his death.

He decided to park his car in an area that was not readily observable, but still fairly accessible in the event he had to make a fast exit. For this situation he took his favorite car, a 2003 Buick LaCrosse. It was a good-looking car, but he had put a lot of money into it and that made it one fast and hard driving car as well.

On his way over to Ben's he mulled over the possible events that were to come. If it was a normal meeting concerning their business, he would find Ben in the den. If he were going over there for a fun time then he would find Ben on the veranda, if the weather was nice, or in his fun room, if not. Anyplace else in the house could well mean trouble, big trouble. He was hoping against all hope Ben was in his den or on the veranda.

The rest of the time he spent planning his actions based on what was going on with Ben. He had never felt this way before. Ben was his closest friend and to have these feelings about him was not normal. Then it entered his mind that if this thing went bad and he survived he was then faced with dealing with Ben's dad and his army. If he only wounded Ben, then he may have a chance, but if he ended up killing Ben, then his own life was done. He may be able to run for a while but in time they would find him and he would pay.

He thought seriously about just turning west and heading out of the Chicago area. Just get out while the getting was good. But that would do no good. If Ben is mad enough, he'll spend any amount of money to find you and get payback. No, it's best to face this now and get it over with. If he survives then he'll deal with that at that time. If not, he has nothing to worry about. What a hell of a way to start a day.

As he came closer to Ben's place, he felt his level of alertness increase. He knew he was in trouble with Ben and from Ben's past history, there was a good possibility that he would not leave Ben's place alive. He hated the idea of having to defend himself against Ben, but he also did not want to die. His mind was set. If the right scenario presents itself, he is safe. If not, then he's ready to defend himself.

It was almost four o'clock that afternoon when Jewell parked down the street from Ben's. He had picked a spot that was somewhat hidden from Ben's house view and headed in the right direction to get him to the Interstate and heading out of the Chicago area as fast as possible. After parking he sat there for several minutes watching to see if any other cars came through the area or if any were parked in places they should not be. It appeared to be clear, so he checked his Glocks and started walking toward the house.

For one guy, Ben's house was huge. In actuality it was around ten thousand square feet sitting on two acres of manicured gardens and lawn. It was a single floor ranch style house with a three-car garage at the front, serviced by a circular driveway. All three garage doors were closed and no cars were in the driveway.

The front double doors were almost dead center of the front facade of the house, solid and a good six feet wide. As he approached the door, he double checked his guns and made sure they were loose and ready to be used. He rang the doorbell and Ben came onto the intercom.

Jewell took a deep breath and then said. "Yeah, Ben its Jewell."

There was a long silence before Ben answered him. "Come on in, I'm in my bedroom."

That's a bad place. He heard the electronic lock click and reached for the door knob and opened the door and stepped in and to the side. He did not want his body silhouetted by the door opening. He closed the door and made sure it was locked with the dead bolt and started toward the bedroom.

The hall to the bedroom branched off of the front foyer and ran down the front of the house, it serviced all four bedrooms. Each bedroom was to the left as you walked down the hall and each was around twenty by twenty feet in size with a sliding glass door going out onto the veranda. The right side of the hall entered the three-car garage from two separate doors located at equal distances down the hall from the foyer.

Ben's bedroom was the last room on the left and was actually twice the size of the others. It actually wrapped around the veranda and when you came out the sliding door you would be looking across the pool to the back of the playroom and den area. The setup in that room was perfect for an ambush. He would have blankets over him and who knew how many guns he could have under the covers.

When he got to the bedroom door he knocked and Ben called out to him to come on in. He pushed the door open and stepped back just when the first round hit the edge of the door as it swung open. Ben then started stitching rounds through the wall toward where Jewell was standing. Jewell dropped down low and moved in through the door and then opened up on Ben with both Glocks. The first three rounds hit him almost body mass center. Ben just kept on firing, even as Ben was going back onto the bed.

Jewell stepped around the end of the

bed and cut loose with everything he had. His clips went dry and he exchanged clips and opened up on him again. There was going to be only one survivor. It was either Jewell or Ben and right now it looked like Ben was going down for the count.

Ben finally stopped moving and Jewell moved around to the top of the bed and with his left Glock pointed at Ben's forehead and pulled the trigger. Nothing, that clip was empty. He then brought the right-hand Glock up and repeated the shot and this one went off and hit Ben's forehead dead center.

He dropped his arms and stood there looking down on Ben. His guts were twisting and he was sure he was going to vomit, but he didn't have time. He had to think fast and move even faster. He wasn't worried about anyone reporting gun shots because the bedroom was insulated on three sides by the rest of the house and the remaining side was made up of glass doors that opened on to a swimming pool area and gave a view of the valley beyond that.

He walked out to his car and drove it back to the house and then went back inside after parking his car backed up to the middle garage door. In the bedroom he wrapped Ben in a blanket and carried him out to the car and placed him in the trunk. He then went back into the house to Ben's den where he found the cash, he knew Ben kept in his desk, bottom left drawer. He figured there was around fifty thousand dollars in the bundle, which would support him for some time. He then closed the house up and left by the front door, locking it behind him.

Once in the car he decided to stop by Bickle's and pick up a garbage can to place Ben's body in. He then went back home and backed his car into the garage and opened the trunk. He placed the garbage can alongside the car and then pulled Ben, in the blanket, out of the trunk and dropped him feet first into the garbage can. He then took a roll of masking tape and taped the lid to the garbage can making sure it was sealed. With that he placed the garbage can back in the trunk and closed it and went into the house.

He immediately took a shower and ran his clothes through the washer and dryer. Then he packed his suitcases and prepared to leave town. He had two stops to make on his way out of town. One was to stop by his bank and withdraw his funds totaling seventy-one thousand dollars and then to his second bank, cleaning out his safety deposit box which held one hundred thirty-three thousand dollars.

All in all, he would be leaving town with a little more than a quarter of a million dollars. He had no idea where he wanted to go or how far he wanted to go. All he knew was he had to get the hell out of there and do it now. Right now, his life was about as worthless as a fire on a hot August day.

He made sure he had several guns in his suitcases along with every box of ammo for those guns he had in the place. He loaded the car and opened the garage door and drove out.

Just south of Tinley Park was Interstate 80 and he headed that direction. He knew right then and there that going east was simply driving into additional trouble. Ben's family was too well known out that way. No, he had to go west and go as far and as fast as he could. Yes, going west was the best overall for him. There were few if any people out there that would be a worry or problem for him. He was financially set and he could move much more freely out west than there in his own territory.

Time, it was time that was his greatest problem and he did not have that much to waste, he had to take the best advantage of what time he did have.

That was a little over a week ago and here he was crossing the panhandle of Idaho heading into Washington. He was on Interstate 90 and knew that he was heading toward Seattle. Seattle was a bad place for him to go. No, he would need to avoid Seattle and the perfect place to do that was eastern Washington.

There he was in Washington State and he still had Ben in his trunk. Why he hadn't gotten rid of the body by now he was not sure, he just hadn't found that place, that location where he felt comfortable leaving the body, in a place where it would never be found.

He stopped at a gas station on the outskirts of Spokane and got a map of the state and started to study it. After a few minutes he knew he wanted to go as far west as Ellensburg and then head south on Interstate 82 to Yakima. Man do they have odd place names out here.

Once in the Yakima area he would then find State Route 12 and head west. That would put him well south of the Seattle/Tacoma area and into a less populous part of the state. He figured that he was looking at five to seven hours of driving time.

His problem was that he was starting to smell Ben inside his car and he needed to locate a place where he could dispose of him.

He bought a six pack of Coke and some snacks and headed for State Route 12. From Spokane he continued west on Interstate 90. This country was much like that to the east of the Rockies' and it made him think that there was nothing else out here in the west.

As he approached Ellensburg, he found Interstate 82 and turned south going toward Yakima. He was getting hungry and decided to stop over in Yakima for lunch and then make the final run to the western side of the Cascade Mountain Range.

His timing was just right and he figured he would get over the mountains and to Interstate 5 by four o'clock that afternoon where he would turn south and then locate a place to sack out for a few hours. He still had to find a place to dump Ben.

The weather was great and traffic moderate and he made it to the State Route 12 junction in good time. He then headed across the mountain to western Washington and hopefully some place where he could make the drop.

As he traveled west on highway 12, he

noted that the landscape started to change. He was heading toward White Pass and beyond that a place called Packwood. The numbers of pine trees were increasing. He had been seeing pines all along the way from Montana to now, but now a newer tree was starting to appear.

He had no idea what they were, but then remembered seeing the same tree as he entered the Rockies'. The forest land became a rich green and the numbers of rivers and stream increased, it was a wonderland of change and he was starting to relax and take in the scenery. He lost track of the time and before he knew it, he was going down the other side, and approaching the small town of Packwood, about ninety miles from Interstate 5.

After another hour and a half, he was approaching Interstate 5 and needed to go south. Within an hour he was approaching the small town of Castle Rock and decided to find a motel. In this part of the state there was nothing but trees. Miles after miles of forest land, the perfect location for disposing of a body. It was about three o'clock that afternoon and everything was working out just fine.

He found a motel, drove into town, and found a hardware store where he bought a shovel. He then went back to the motel parking lot and started looking at his map. He found what he thought was the perfect location. It was off a road called the Jackson Highway, just north of a rest areas three miles back north on Interstate 5. There was a small road named Hill Creek that shared a junction with Roger's Road, and Jackson Highway. He would turn south away from the Jackson Highway. About a quarter of a mile south there was what looked like a logging or service road of some kind that looked perfect for his purposes.

So, he headed out and sure enough he had it figured right. Once on the logging road all he had to do was pick a location and get it done. He finally came to an area that looked perfect. The undergrowth along the road was around three feet high and there were a number of large trees on the hillside to his right, a perfect place for Ben to spend eternity. He planted Ben at the base of a tree. Maybe the grave was too shallow, but that's the way it had to be. No one would ever find him here anyway, whether he was buried or not.

When he finished, he threw the garbage can and lid up into the brush and sent the shovel in the opposite direction. Then he headed back to the motel and sacked out for the night. The next morning, he knew that Jewell Scarpone had to disappear and so he set about planning that end.

Just before noon the following day he drove north on I-5 to the Jackson Highway overpass and then turned around and headed south on I-5 to the southbound Toutle River Rest Stop.

As he pulled into the rest stop, he looked the area over, found a good spot to park and left his car. If he was lucky no one would question it for several days and when they did, he would be long gone and untraceable. It was a good plan, but as with many good plans, some things don't work out right. He needed a gullible individual to come by and give him a ride, someone who would not question his being there, without a ride. Jewell had worked up a cover story and he was ready.

About an hour later a car pulled in with a lone male driving. As the guy walked to the restroom Jewell started moving toward his car. As he watched the guy, he could tell he really needed to go bad. Yeah, this would be the perfect guy. Doesn't plan that well and not built like he would be a problem for Jewell to deal with.

Five minutes later Phillip Morles was walking back to his car when Jewell approached him. They spent about five minutes talking when Jewell asked if he could get a ride. The guy made some smart-ass remark about Jewell not shooting him down the road, to which Jewell reacted with surprise and then started to laugh.

Jewell quickly shot back. "Actually, my mom always told me never to take a ride with a stranger."

They both laughed.

Phil had decided that this guy appeared to be fine and agreed. He would take him south as far as he wanted to go until they hit L.A. With that they left the rest stop heading south.

Chapter Four

THE DISCOVERY

It had been more than a week since old Benito had last seen or talked to his son Ben and that was unusual. He had his driver take him by Ben's place to see if he was all right. In his line of business, you don't go long without contacting someone close to you to insure they're all right. What he found in his sons' home was enough to cause even the worst of his enemies to shudder.

When they entered the house, he could immediately smell the dried and decomposing blood. He got to the bed room and saw the aftermath of the battle. It was obvious that someone had been seriously hurt and, in all probability, killed judging from the amount of blood in the room.

When Benito saw the room, he froze where he stood. His driver saw the old man's reactions and tried to help him only to be slammed against the wall and screamed at.

Benito was instantly in a state of rage and he was in a killing mood. "Where's my son?"

Benito then screamed at his driver and bodyguard. "Find him and do it now."

The old man's driver and bodyguard ran out of the room to the nearest phones and called a number of their people to get over to Ben's place immediately. By this time the old man was screaming and crying. He knew, he knew without a doubt that Ben was dead. The old guy had seen gun battle sites before and could read them like a book.

Benito was screaming and beating on the wall. "Who did this? I damn them to hell and when I get my hands on them, they will take weeks to die. I'll cut their soul out of them one piece at a time. If anyone in the business is tied up in this I'll find out and kill them and their whole family. If I have to live another hundred years, I will find them and I will take my revenge."

Even under the circumstances of his apparent son's death the old man was still thinking. As members of his organization arrived, they were assigned to cleaning up the house of any illegal contraband or evidence that could tie his son and himself to any criminal activity.

Even the bedroom was gone over making sure that nothing could draw the police to the family. Everything had to be cleansed before calling in the police.

Benito's Bodyguard then pointed out the guns, "Benito, what about the guns?"

Benito turned and looked at the guns on the bed and floor. "Leave them many people have guns that shouldn't have them. Ben was a big boy and besides that, what can they do to Ben now. No, leave them. They can make what they want of them, I don't care."

Though they were his enemy, the authorities were called and an official report was made as to the probability of the death of his son. Next, they addressed the task of trying to determine who was there and where his son's body had been taken. By this time, they knew that Jewell was missing as well and so was his car. None of Ben's cars were gone or even moved.

Tinley Park police knew they had a touchy situation on their hands. They clearly were not pleased with the identification of the victim. And, now the father was in the hunt for someone, anyone to nail for what had happened to his son.

Being Sicilian and Catholic, Benito's first need was to bring his son home and give him a proper burial. The second task was to find the person or persons who did this and make them pay slowly for every bullet that hit his son.

It was old Benito who had determined that Jewell was involved in this thing up to his neck. He knew only two types of ammunition had been used at the scene, nine-millimeter and .40 caliber weapons. He knew his son favored the nine-millimeter and he knew that Jewell favored the .40 caliber. That made it simple for him. Jewell was involved and if not, he would know who was.

Word had been passed around the families that there had been no hits asked for or approved through the mob. This was a personal, one on one situation and Ben had come out on the wrong end. When they get Jewell or whomever, they will more than wish the fight had been the other way around.

The word spread across the country. All the families in the New York and east coast areas had been notified that Jewell was being hunted. The old man knew Jewell would not go that way, but they had contacts throughout the country and any information they got would be helpful. The southern region of the country was the same way. The New Orleans family was well connected throughout the area from Florida out through Arizona. All that was left was the west coast, and in short order every mob connection from Vancouver BC to San Diego was on the lookout for Jewell.

Anywhere in the nation where organized crime had a foothold or had any interest was on the alert for Jewell. The reward was substantial and the demand for a live delivery was part of the deal.

When the machine was turned on it ran nonstop. It never rested and it never tired. It just kept on cranking day in and day out. Nothing but nothing was going to stop it. Jewell was a marked man and even the authorities felt they would not be able to prevent the Chicago family from getting their hands on him.

The search took on new life with the

discovery of Ben's body in Washington State three weeks later. Benito, the old man, Cipozzio flew out to Washington himself to recover his son's body. He was advised by the local authorities that it was best he not view his son's body, but Benito needed to know, with his own eyes, that his beloved son was in fact dead.

It was bad enough that these hicks out here in the western back country had his body, but to be telling him what he could or should do was not acceptable. He was there to take his son home and he was there to see with his own eyes that his son was dead. That confirmation was paramount and it would be the foundation of all the activity that would follow.

As he walked into the local funeral home the proprietor met him and gave him his condolences. It was a solemn moment, one that the old man would honor for the sake of his son. He was taken into the viewing room and when the proprietor approached the casket to open it Benito waved him away and asked him to leave. When the man was gone Benito, with a slight motion of his hand, had his associate open the casket for him.

As the casket opened the impact of

seeing his son gray colored and his face damaged as it was caused him to drop to his knees. The mortuary had done a good job preparing his son for this meeting and for that Benito was grateful. He advised his associate to pay the man double the presented fees.

With that business now finished, arrangements were made for the transportation of Ben's body back to Tinley Park, a trip his father would take riding by his son's side on a chartered plane.

Once the formal claiming of the body was done and they were in-route back to Illinois, the word went out that the reward for finding Jewell had just tripled. It would include a twenty-five percent bonus when he was brought in alive, without the authorities knowing about it. When they were through, Jewell's body would simply appear somewhere out of state and that would be the end of it.

Then Benito upped the ante. Anyone caught helping Jewell in any way to avoid them would pay with their lives. It was a Cart Blanche order and one that would carry a hefty financial reward. Whether the individual or individuals knew of Jewell's situation or not the old man wanted them dead. Everyone was going to pay for even so much as knowing Jewell. Around Tinley Park those who had known Jewell were now denying any knowledge of who he was or where he may have gone. In effect they had completely isolated him.

They knew that he had been in a motel in a small town just a mile away from where the body had been found. The manager of that motel received visitors two days after Ben's body had been claimed by his father.

As the men entered the lobby, the clerk knew that they meant business. They asked for the manager and she called her boss. As he walked up to the counter the smaller of the two men asked him. "Could you tell us if a Jewell Scarpone registered at this motel within the last month?"

The manager could see that these people meant business and decided not to argue with them. He advised them that Jewell arrived and was given room number twenty-two and that he had been there just two days and had left without checking out.

He gave them the description of his car and told them that the police had done a complete search of the room and had also recovered the car in the rest stop just north of the town.

After answering a number of additional questions concerning Jewell and whether he had anyone else with him they left. The manager walked back to his office and called the investigator working the case and advised him as to what had just happened. He last saw them driving off in a 2003 black Cadillac with Washington plates. He provided a full description of both men and hung up.

At this point the authorities knew that Benito was looking for Jewell. They had his car and it was full of blood and other evidence that tied him to the killing back in Tinley Park.

They knew by the fact that Jewell's car had been parked at the rest stop that he had gotten a ride with someone else. Either a stranger or someone he knew and had met him at that location. From all that, it was not hard to determine that he was heading south, probably toward California.

Benito's people had made the same determinations and were fanning out all along the Interstate watching for Jewell. They were sure that he had gotten a ride from some unlucky soul who would end up paying the ultimate price for his Good Samaritan deed, as innocent as it was.

Each and every bit of information concerning the hunt for Jewell was relayed back to Benito. It was put together with everything else they knew and then gone over in detail to try and develop a greater understanding of where Jewell was heading and what his plans were.

It was then that Benito's bodyguard advised him, after completing the search of Ben's house and before calling the police, they had discovered that there was some fifty thousand dollars in cash missing from Ben's den desk. Other than that, the only sign that anyone had been in the house was in Ben's bedroom.

The bodyguard then started to speculate. "Do you think it was just a robbery?"

Benito sat there. "No, it was not a robbery. Anyone in that line would know better than to hit Ben. No, that money was known to be there by Ben's killer and when the fight was over, he went to Ben's den and took it to finance his run from us. Anyone robbing Ben would have torn the place apart to find that money. Also, Jewell would have known where it was at."

He was even surer that Jewell was involved and probably was the killer. What probably hurt the most was the fact that Ben and Jewell had been so close all these years and now Jewell had taken his sons life. It made no difference what the circumstances were, it made no difference whether Ben had started the fight or not, the fact was that Jewell had killed Benito's son and Jewell would pay the ultimate price.

At that point Benito did something that clearly communicated his intentions for Jewell. He ordered that Jewell's home be burned and anything that he owned or had an interest in was to be destroyed as well. He wanted the act done within the next twenty-four hours.

That night two men pulled up in front of Jewell's home, left their car and approached the house and broke in, five minutes later they came out and drove away. About the time they turned the first corner a block away the whole of the house burst into flames and was nearly totally consumed before the fire department arrived.

It was the first in a long list of vengeance that Benito would rain down on Jewell in every way he possibly could. There was no longer any doubt in his mind that he knew who had killed his son. All that was left was to find him and then finish the fight. That was all he was living for. He wanted, no he had to see Jewell's blood and he would not be satisfied with anything less than Jewell being presented to him alive.

Chapter Five

OREGON COAST

As they drove out of Lincoln City south bound, Jewell was back to watching the ocean. This part of Oregon was made up of a varied landscape. The mountains ran into the ocean, dropping off in the form of high cliffs. There were sand dunes between the highway and the ocean that were as big as mountains. Where they came from was a mystery to Jewell. Then there were areas where the highway ran right along the ocean.

The vistas in these locations were as varied as the terrain itself. As you looked out on to the Pacific it would reflect the sky and amplify the majesty of the scenery. Whether high, driving along the cliffs or down low and skirting the beaches the scene changed continuously. Jewell was sure that no matter what the weather conditions the view from the road was mind boggling. In one short mile you could see two and three different vistas and each one was as wondrous as the one before. Phil watched as Jewell sat with his eyes glued to the window looking at the ocean and the beaches as they passed by them.

Phil had the distinct feeling that there was something wrong. He was not ready to address the issue with Jewell, but he had that deep down inside gut feeling that he had better not wait too long.

South of Lincoln City you start to come to a number of his favorite locations and one of those at the top of his list was the Newport Great Aquarium.

Phil looked over at Jewell. "Jewell, you interested in sea life?"

Jewell had been in a deep state of thought when Phil asked and he sat up and looked back at Phil. "What did you say?"

Phil saw the blank look in Jewell's face and then slowly repeated his question. "Jewell, are you interested in sea life like at an aquarium?"

Jewell sat there taking in what Phil had asked and then seemed to comprehend. "Oh, yes I would like to see something like that, sounds great to me."

"Good there's a great one just a short distance out of Newport, to the south of it." Phil replied.

As they traveled south, they passed through Depoe Bay without stopping. Jewell slipped back into his isolation and watched the ocean go by.

They finally came into Newport, and drove through the main part of town and crossed the bridge where they turned into the aquarium parking lot. Phil found a spot toward the far corner of the lot. As they exited the car Jewell kept looking around. It was not the look of someone seeing something for the first time, but a watchful look. A look that was of a person watching for something to happen or take place, something he didn't want to see happen.

They walked on into the aquarium and started walking through the displays and observation areas. Jewell had never seen anything like it before. He was totally engrossed in everything. He could hardly believe that all these creatures came from the ocean just across the highway and not more than a mile away. He looked at everything and for the time being he could separate himself from the worries that were following him.

It was while they were walking through the main aquarium glass tunnel that Jewell became quiet and seemed to turn inward. As he looked through the glass, he could almost imagine himself there in that realm slowly cruising along with little apparent effort. With all his problems that appeared to be the most secure and problem free environment he had ever seen.

At one point they sat down on a park bench and Phil looked at Jewell. Phil knew he had to ask now and there could be no delay. Something was wrong and he knew it and needed to have it out in the open. "Please forgive me, but I just have to ask you. Is there anything wrong? I mean if there is, would being able to tell someone about it help in any way? Would it help to tell someone what is going on?"

Jewell appeared irritated and then let that quickly pass. He sat there for a few seconds watching the crowd walk by and started to say something, he caught himself and stopped. He looked at Phil. Jewell then started to pick his words carefully and continued. "Not really. It's just that I'm heading out to start over and there is always stress and worry involved in something like that."

Phil sat there watching him and nodded his head. "Yeah, I know what you mean, had the same feeling after my divorce." They sat there quietly for another few minutes when Jewell turned to Phil. "Hey, where did you grow up?"

Phil wasn't expecting that question and had to sit back and get himself organized before starting. "Me, oh I was born and raised in Everett. My father worked for the city. Believe it or not, he was a traffic engineer."

Jewell sat up and looked at Phil. "You mean one of those guys that design our roads and street?"

Phil laughed and replied, "Yeah that was my dad."

Jewell was clearly interested and responded back. "Wow, I always wondered how they came off with some of their solutions to the traffic problems I've seen over the years."

Phil smiled as he thought back to his

father and those times. "Yeah, I used to ask him why they did something one way or the other. He always said that it was part solution and part money."

Jewell tipped his head. "How was that?"

Phil continued his trip back into his memory and his times with his father. "Well, he would say that they would address a particular problem, come up with the best solution and when they were done, they would cost it out. It usually turned out that the city manager would not want to spend that kind of money from the budget for that particular job. Sometimes it didn't work out right and was worse than before they started.

"It drove dad nuts. Especially when the public and friends started in on him about the shoddy job they did on this project or that, made him mad as hell. I think that was part of the reason he died so young."

Jewell could feel the memories flowing through Phil at the moment. "Oh, what happened?"

Phil hadn't thought of his dad and his death for a long time and he felt he needed to tell Jewell about it. "The usual thing, he got up one morning and headed off for work. By the time he got to his office he wasn't feeling well. He told his partner that he needed to go into the break room and lay down for a couple of minutes. Twenty minutes later they went to check on him and he was dead, turned out to be a bad heart."

Jewell could feel the loss radiating from Phil. "How old were you?"

Phil could feel the sorrow welling up in him it had been such a long time ago. "I was fifteen at the time."

Jewell reached over and put his hand on Phil' shoulder. "That's one hell of an age to lose your dad at."

Phil continued on. "Oh, it wasn't too hard, mom was a teacher at the Everett High School and she was able to provide for us. With dad's insurance and pension benefits we had no real money issues. The hard part was adjusting to him not being there."

Jewell's interest was pricked and he had to ask. "Did your mother ever remarry?"

Phil smiled and continued on. "Yeah, she did, about two years after my younger sister graduated from high school Mom and one of her fellow teachers tied the knot."

Jewell kept reaching out to learn more and understand. "How did you feel about

103

that?"

Phil smiled again and continued. "Oh, he's a great guy. She deserved to have a good man and he is just that. The family took him in right away. He had lost his wife some ten years earlier and had three kids. It has made for a great family story. Both sides miss their respective parent and we all realize that and honor both of them as we should. No, mom is doing just fine."

Phil then turned and looked at Jewell. "How about your family?"

Jewell seemed to pull back a little. "Me!"

Phil continued to push the issue. "Yes you."

Jewell had not thought about his home life for so long and it was a hell of a lot different from what Phil had just told him. "Well, my old man was a fair enough dad. Not too bright, I mean he quit school after the ninth grade and was a laborer his whole life. He worked hard and we were never short on anything in particular. He was hard on mom though. Used to get loaded up on the weekend and come home and punch her out once in a while.

"My brother and I couldn't do much

about it, mom made us stay out of the fights. She took it from him and then went on and did her job as our mom. Never saw any woman anywhere like her. Guess that's why I never married, couldn't find a woman like her that could put up with me.

"When I was seventeen, we were just hanging around home, it was late when dad came home that night drunk as, well, he was drunk and he started in on her. I was sitting there in the living room when he pasted her with his fist right in the middle of her face. Blood flew everywhere. I started out of my seat and he turned and looked at me and pointed his finger at me. Just then my older brother, he was nineteen then, hit him from behind and we both went after him.

"Mom was down for the count and not able to stop our assault and we cut loose on him. Before we were done, we broke both his arms. We had him down on the floor with our knees on his chest and we told him. No more. He even so much as touched her wrong and we would kill him and dispose of what was left. I then told him that I thought the Cipozzio family would be willing to help do that job.

"The look on his face was pure terror.

He was so scared. I realized that just the name of my friend Ben's family scared most grown men. I then promised him, dad I mean it. I know the family and even if I had to join them to get their help with him I would.

"Never, never again would he hurt our mom, or I swore he would pay for it. That ended it. His arms healed and he never touched mom again. Not too long after that my brother and I moved out. Dad died of cancer two years later. Mom followed him three years later from cancer."

Phil sat there and asked. "How's your brother doing today?"

Jewell looked down at the ground between his feet and nervously shuffled them. "Ted? He was killed in a street shooting two years ago, took a round in the head. Two rival gang members got into a shoot out on a street corner, he walked around the corner of the building when they started shooting and he took the round. He didn't even know what hit him."

Phil took a deep breath and then sat back again. "Damn, that's terrible. Sorry about that Jewell. They ever get the guys?"

Jewell continued, "Yeah, they got like six of them and were able to identify the one who shot the round that killed Ted. The kid that shot him was only seventeen years old. What a waste. They sent him off to life without parole. They should have left him on the street. He would have been taken care of in a much straighter forward manner and more permanently."

"I thought you said that your mom died out here in Seattle?" Phil asked.

"Yeah, she did, that was three years ago." Replied Jewell.

They sat there a few minutes and Phil leaned forward and looked straight at Jewell; "Jewell, you with the mob?"

Jewell sat there like he didn't even hear the question then looked at Phil. "Kind of Phil, I'm not a real member. I guess you would call me an associate of sorts. My best friend Ben is the son of one of the family bosses in the Chicago area."

Phil sat back, "Oh."

Jewell anticipated Phil's next question. "You want to know if I'm in trouble with the mob."

Phil nodded his head. "Well, are you?"

Jewell knew the time had come for the truth with this man, he owed it to him. "Yeah, Phil I am. In fact, I'm in so much trouble that when they find me, and they will, they will kill me. That's not a guess that is a fact."

Phil felt himself flush. "Wow!"

At this point Phil was thinking that he shouldn't be involved in this. He looked at Jewell and just sat there. Jewell sat up straight, "Phil, get your ass to your car and leave now. No need in you being involved in this thing. If they find you with me, I have no doubt that you will get it as well. You're a great guy and I just don't want you on my conscience even if it was for a short time."

Jewell looked like he was ready to leave when Phil reached out and took his arm. "Look, I said I would take you as far as L.A. Well, that's what I'm going to do."

Phil's mind was exploding. *What the hell do you think you're doing anyway? You fat headed idiot. Damn man I have never seen anyone do anything as dumb as you just did. Let him go. Get the hell out of here and do it now.*

As each minute passed Phil became more determined. "Look Jewell I don't know what you did, but right now this is not the place to leave you. No, you need to get someplace that is more suited to you. More of an environment that you're used to. L.A. is that place, can't get much closer to being like Chicago here on the coast."

Phil finally asked the big question. "Now, what are they after you for?"

Jewell looked at Phil and simply said. "Theft."

It wasn't a lie he had taken the fifty thousand dollars out of Ben's den desk. He thought it best not to tell Phil about the killing, at least not now.

Phil was not accepting that story. "Do you mean to tell me that they would kill over a theft?"

Jewell backed what he had said up with. "Phil, they would kill a person and have killed people for much less. Once on their list, the only solution is death, yours preferably."

Phil continued to pursue the issue. "What are your chances of getting away from them?"

Jewell stayed with him. "Right now, not bad. Tomorrow, who knows? My problem is that it's the Cipozzio family that is after me."

Phil stopped for a second, he knew that name. "The Cipozzio family, I've heard of them. They're big stuff back east around the Chicago area, is that right?"

Jewell smiled when he looked at Phil, this kid had guts. "That they are, my friend that they are. The old man is a mean son-of-a-gun and he never gives up. My only hope is that he dies before they find me."

Phil was looking for answers by this time. "How about the police?"

Jewell shrugged his shoulders. "What about them?"

Phil raised his hand, palm up. "Well, if you give yourself up to them then they could protect you."

Jewell half way laughed at that and replied. "Yeah, right they're about as much protection as Benito Cipozzio himself is right now. If they lock me up then I can expect a soldier to come into the jail and kill me there on the spot.

Phil found it hard to believe what Jewell was saying. "You mean that someone would get himself arrested and put in jail just to kill you?"

Jewell looked at Phil. "Yeah, they do it all the time."

Phil found that hard to accept and said so. "That's crazy. All right, what are we going to do?"

Jewell was obviously surprised by

Phil's question. "Phil, are you serious about sticking with me to L.A.?"

It was time for Phil to make that final decision, whether he should stick it out with Jewell or run like hell anywhere as long as it was away from Jewell and his troubles, but he answered. "Yes."

By this time Jewell was clearly measuring his situation up and trying to determine if he had a chance with Phil running with him. "Then we need to work out some kind of system where we can keep an eye out and give ourselves the best chance of seeing the hunters coming. Phil, do you know how to handle a gun?"

Phil suddenly was faced with the reality of what he was working himself into. "Oh boy I don't know if I like that question."

The predator in Jewell came out of its hiding place and started measuring the mettle of his friend. "Phil, you need a fighting chance in the event they find you with me, without some ability handling a gun, you're just fresh meat to those hunting me."

The question had caught Phil off guard and he was recoiling from the implications. "Yeah, but, aw crap. I don't shoot guns. I don't even know how to hold one. Hell, if you handed one to me right now I would problem end up holding it with the barrel pointing at me."

Jewell almost started laughing, partly because of the humor involved in what Phil had said and the other part because of the nervousness of the moment on Phil. "Calm down, I was just asking. All right, leave the guns to me."

Phil almost stood up. "You have guns with you?"

Jewell was looking around, trying to calm Phil down. "Yes, I do, but stop talking so loudly. You're going to get us in hot water and that we don't need right now."

Phil almost shoved his fist down his throat trying to control himself. He was really panicking and Jewell was losing control of the situation.

Jewell stood up and took Phil by the elbow and started walking him toward the car. "Phil, let's get back to the car and we can finish our conversation there."

Back at the car things were not much better. Phil was coming apart at the seams and Jewell could only wait until he calmed down. All Phil could do was sit there and shake. It wasn't the fear for his life that was bothering him it was the whole thing hitting him all at once. Yes, and he had also told Jewell that he would not leave him stranded here in Newport.

What was the matter with me? He thought.

Finally, Phil turned to Jewell. "Tell me the whole damn thing and don't leave anything out?"

With that Jewell went into the whole story from beginning to end. An hour later all Phil could do was sit there and stare at Jewell.

Then he asked. "You drove him all the way out here to bury him?"

Jewell's eyes opened wide and he realized that after all he had just told him he focused in on the trip west. "Yeah, I had to get out of town fast and I just headed west. By the time I decided I wanted to get rid of the body I was driving through open country and there were no real places to stash the body.

"Finally, when I got over the mountains and into western Washington the landscape was just the right place for dumping the body. I thought I found a place where he would never be found.

"Hell, within a few days he was found and here I am running for my life. Actually, I

113

was running when I left the Chicago area. The fact that I was in the house at the time Ben was killed is reason enough for old Benito to have me killed, whether I killed Ben or not."

The two of them sat there looking out across the parking lot as cars came and went. Neither man had any idea what the other was thinking. Jewell was trying to plan his next move and that depended on what Phil finally decided to do. If Phil bailed on him then Jewell would have to make it out of the Newport area and go it alone. If Phil decided to stay with him then he would have to work that into his planning. This was not turning out the way he had originally planned.

Finally, Phil had been able to compose himself enough to continue on in this pursuit of the truth. "Jewell, how many people have you killed over the years?"

He sat there looking at Phil. He had come to like Phil and knew that he had put him into a tight spot, one that would probably cost him his life "Truthfully Phil, around twelve."

Phil put his hand to his mouth and sat back turning his head toward Jewell. "That's counting this, Ben?"

Jewell stopped and thought for a

minute, he was doing a mental inventory of all his jobs. "No, counting Ben it's thirteen."

Phil was beyond the point of reality by this time. "And, you were not arrested for the others?"

Jewell thought for a second, "Yeah, that's right not once. No, they never fingered me on any of them."

Phil couldn't help himself and said sarcastically. "So, how do I die, at your hands or theirs?"

After several minutes of thinking, Jewell reached over and touched Phil's shoulder. "Listen, I'm not the most honorable or honest guy in the world, but I'm also not the biggest jerk. My not telling you what you were getting into was wrong. I felt that if I told you then you would have run and I would still be back there in that rest stop.

"I promise you this. You have nothing to fear from me. Phil, please understand, I will, in time, pay for killing Ben, but I swear to you here and now you will not pay as well. Do you understand me?"

Phil was looking Jewell straight in the eyes and he knew then and there that this man would honor his promise. "Yeah, I do Jewell, you hungry?"

That almost made Jewell hit Phil. He then smiled and raised both hands in surrender. "I could eat a fence post right now."

Phil started the car and pulled it into gear and started to back out of the parking spot. "Great, then I suggest we move on down the road and find a good place to eat."

Jewell felt a load lift off him. "That's fine with me."

Phil then asked. "Oh, Jewell, thanks for being upfront with me, it helps."

Jewell looked out the window toward the ocean. "Should have some time ago Phil, some time ago."

They left the lot and pulled back on to 101 and continued south. Phil had noticed that Jewell's left hand was twitching a little, not much, but every few seconds it twitched. Could just be nerves or something like that. He was under a lot of stress and that could be good or bad.

He would have to keep a close watch on him and if need be, make a run for it. Right now, he felt safe, but knew that under conditions like this anything was possible. His survival was depending on his ability to read Jewell.

They finally found a nice restaurant down the road about ten miles and stopped in to eat. They found a booth at the back of the main dining room that overlooked the beach. As they sat there Jewell was focused on the ocean, something kept drawing him to it. He had been bitten by the saltwater bug. It's called that because when someone falls in love with the beach and ocean, that is what they act like, and he was bitten hard.

Jewell continued to look out across the sand at the ocean. "You know I could easily live right here, right on that beach the rest of my life. It's the most pleasant thing I have ever seen."

Yeah, he was bitten by the saltwater bug all right, Phil thought and then he said. "I know what you mean, but you should be here in the winter and during a storm. That pleasant serene seascape turns gray and mean. It will kill you in seconds, given the chance."

Jewell nodded his head. He understood the wild, the life of the survivor. "I don't doubt that one bit, but that doesn't take away from its beauty and serenity. Look, this is a dangerous world we live in, much of what we see as beautiful can be and is highly dangerous.

"Take the tiger. That, to me is the most beautiful animal walking the face of the earth. I would love to have one as a pet. But I also know that if I had one as a pet, I run a risk of it turning on me. Not because it hates me, but because that is its nature. So, I have to make that decision.

"That animal will live by its nature and circumstances. It may have nothing to do with me or it could be exactly because of me. Whatever the cause, the animal will react or respond to its environment and that may include attacking and killing the one person that loves it the most.

"Do I want to take the risk or not? It's that simple. If I take the risk and he turned, then it's my problem not the tigers. The only reason I don't have one is that if it did turn, they would probably kill it and that would be my fault as well.

"No, whether dangerous or not, that does not diminish the beauty of a tiger, the majesty of a mountain, or the magnitude of the ocean. It's all relative. You accept the hazard with the benefits. I'm sure the people who live here understand that and still they stay. And that is because they love it and have determined that the risk is worth the benefits."

Phil's mouth literally dropped open and he found he could not say a thing, Jewell was right. And, Phil was impressed with Jewell's outlook on life. He could never have voiced it any better and in all probability couldn't even come close. Jewell appreciated life and in his line of work life is something that becomes precious and treasured.

By this time their meals had come and they settled in to enjoy the food and some good conversation. It had been a long time since Jewell had this feeling and was this relaxed. In just a couple of days he had gained more than he had anticipated. His meeting up with Phil, that is.

Outside the restaurant just pulling in off of 101 was a long black low Cadillac with two occupants. They slid down the lane between the parking lanes checking each car, trying to make a determination as to if their prey were there.

Both men had been tracking a cold trail since they had left that small town of Castle Rock up in southwestern Washington. They were sure that their prey was somewhere ahead of them or possibly right here in this parking lot.

Jewell and Phil finished their meal and

were walking to the cashier's desk when Jewell looked out the window and slowed to a near stop as he locked in on a dark car moving through the parking lot. Phil almost ran over him. Phil had been thinking about what he owed the cashier and not paying any attention to what Jewell was doing. "What's going on Jewell?"

Jewell's demeanor had changed and he was now in the hunter mode. "Hold it." Jewell moved to his left toward the back of the restaurant but did so in an easy and controlled manner.

Phil instinctively knew that Jewell had gone on alert, but he had no idea what the hell was going on or what was about to happen. "Jewell what is it?"

Jewell reached back and grabbed Phil' arm and firmly moved him in the direction of the back door. "We got company."

He walked back toward the rest rooms and Phil followed him. They stopped at the restroom door and Jewell turned. "There is a car in the parking lot with two guys in it. It's a dark Cadillac with Washington plate. I'm not positive, but my gut tells me that they are not here for a meal, their looking for me."

Phil had an urge to go out front and

take a look, but responded. "What the hell are we going to do? His eyes were those of a deer being caught in the headlights in the dead of night. He was not ready for, nor did he have any idea, as to what he should do.

While Phil waited, Jewell was planning and making preparations. He then looked straight at Phil and told him. "You're going to go to your car and get in and drive away, understand me. Go down the road until you're out of sight of this place and then pull over to the side of the road. Leave your lights on and put the car in park. I'll catch up with you as soon as I can.

"Now listen I may not get there right away. I am going to have to check these two out and make sure they are still in the parking lot when I get to you. So, give me some time. If I do not make it in twenty to thirty minutes, leave. Get the hell out of here and don't stop until you're back home, got me."

Phil turned and grabbed Jewell. "You sure we should split? I mean maybe we would be better off dealing with them together instead of splitting up."

Jewell pushed Phil's hand off his arm. "Listen to me, they're looking for two guys and if you're alone they wouldn't pay any attention to you. They know me, I'm sure of that, but not you. Just take your time, but don't stop. Just walk out to your car, get in and drive away. Not, fast, just like you do every time you leave work, or a restaurant, or whatever." Jewell was looking Phil directly in the eyes and driving the magnitude of the situation deep into Phil. "Now what are you to do?"

Phil responded and repeated what Jewell had told him.

With that Jewell left the restaurant out the back door on to the patio and then down onto the beach and headed south along the sand dunes. Phil stood there watching him turn and head south on the beach. He then turned and slowly walked back to the front of the restaurant where he paid for the meals and walked out the front door right past the car with the two men. As he walked by, he took his wallet out and stuffed the receipt into it along with his change. They paid no attention to him.

As Phil walked toward his car over in the shadows by the building Jewell was waiting silently with two Glocks in his hands to ensure that Phil had no problems with the two men in the black Cad. When Phil got to his car Jewell slipped back down to the beach and headed south.

God, did they see my hand shaking or was I just another person doing what any other person would do day in and day out. Keep calm and do as Jewell told me.

Deep down inside he was excited and had a feeling he had never felt before. It was like riding the highest rollercoaster in the world and doing it while standing.

When he got to the car, he started it and sat there a minute while putting his seat belt on and then pulled out of the parking spot, back past the Cadillac and to the parking lot entrance and then south onto 101. About a half mile down the road, he found a wide spot and pulled over. He came to a stop and turned the motor off and settled in to wait.

That had worked just as Jewell had told him it would. Those two sat there and he walked right by them and they showed no sign of recognition or curiosity toward him. In a way that was fun as hell.

There was no one around and he was also trying to watch his rear-view mirror to see if the Cadillac came out of the parking lot behind him. It was twenty-five minutes later and he was getting more than a little nervous, he was ready to leave.

Almost as if by magic, Jewell came running up to the car and jumped into the back seat and lay down. "All right get going." And, they headed south. Phil paid close attention to his speed and driving habits. He fully expected the Cadillac to appear behind him, but it never did.

It was about forty-five miles from Newport to Florence, Oregon. As they came into Florence Jewell told Phil to pull into the first motel they came to and drive to the back of the lot away from the main office. He would get out there and get a room. Phil was to go on into town and get a room in the next motel he came to. Phil was to register in his own name and then was to call Jewell once he was checked in. Jewell told Phil that he would not be registering under his actual name. That when Phil called the motel to ask for Walter Manning.

Jewell got one of his suit cases and walked off and Phil exited the parking lot back onto 101 and headed for the next motel. Thirty minutes later Phil was in his room and calling the motel that Jewell had checked into. Once he had contacted Jewell, they made plans for the next day. Jewell had checked his motels parking lot and the Cadillac was not there. The same was true for Phil's location.

In the morning they would meet up on the street back of Jewell's motel and then leave town. From then on Jewell planned on riding in the back seat sitting low or laying down. They knew the Cad was in that area and they figured that if they took their time and went slowly, the Cad would move on out and ahead of them. They were right. The two in the Cad moved on south scanning every town, every parking lot, and every attraction looking for their prey.

The hunted had played their first move on the board. They managed to avoid that first move of the hunters and countered with a few moves of their own. The key to their traveling on south was to take it slow and easy. Now they wanted to stop everywhere and see everything and anything. It made no difference, the longer it took them to go a mile the better. They needed the guys in the Cad to move on south ahead of them.

Florence, Oregon to Crescent City, California was about one hundred sixty miles, as the crow flies. On 101 that would translate into almost two hundred miles. So, they planned on it taking them the whole day. Still there was a danger that the guys would turn around and back track on themselves, just in case they had missed Jewell. So, he still rode in the back seat and stayed as low as he could.

They had stopped at a small place on one of the back streets of Florence and had breakfast, and just before noon stopped at another roadside place for lunch. Each time they took precautions to make sure that the Cad was not there when they parked. If it wasn't for the fact that all the stress helped build their hunger levels they may not have stopped to eat. However, they also needed to keep their strength up and not eating would not help.

It was maybe around two o'clock that afternoon when Phil was pulling into a local art gallery that their precautions paid off. It was a left turn across the highway into the parking lot of the gallery when the Cad came into view coming north on the highway. Phil almost turned right in front of them, but managed to stop short of hitting them. The driver looked right at Phil and not knowing what else to do, Phil shrugged his shoulders and then lipped 'I'm sorry' to the driver and he nodded as he drove by.

Phil could hardly contain himself. He

didn't know if he had made the ultimate blunder or if things were going to be just fine. "Jewell, it's them. Damn it's the Cad and I almost ran into them." Just the realization of what had just happened caused Phil to go into a sweat. His hands were shaking and he felt like he could throw up.

Jewell almost came over the back of the front seat. He was almost asleep when Phil had hit the brakes to stop for the Cad, it almost put Jewell on the floor and all he could do was say. "The Cad?" His face flushed and he went for his guns before he was able to regain control and get back onto the seat and get himself oriented.

Phil was looking in his rearview mirror back down the road at the Cad as it continued on north. He was trying to determine if the Cad was going to continue on or turn around. Right now, it was moving on north. "Yeah, I almost ran into them. What should I do?" The cad was still moving north and he was losing sight of it.

Jewell's mind was going at hyper-speed. "Pull into the lot and get out and walk into the gallery. Don't look back or out toward the highway. Just walk into the gallery. Keep your head Phil they have no way of connecting us right now so play it cool. Just pull into a parking spot and get out. Don't sit and wait or do anything like that, just get out and walk into the shop. It's a normal everyday thing and this is your normal everyday stop off."

Phil was not sure what he should do "You sure? You want me to go on into the shop and look around like there was nothing wrong. I don't know if I can do that." He was scared and not thinking clearly.

Jewell snapped back at him. "Yes, damn it, I'm sure you can do it, now get out and do it." Jewell was busy in the back seat doing what, Phil had no idea, but Jewell was preparing for the worst if it came.

Phil pulled into the parking lot and found a parking spot right in front of the shop door. He parked the car and made sure it was in park. Phil left the car and walked over to the door and walked in, once inside he turned and looked back out at the lot. Sure, as hell the Cad was pulling in. Crap, their coming to check on him, what now?

Phil started to count and get control of his action. *Do as I normally do, get a brochure and start to look at it and the works on the wall, act normal as if nothing was out of the ordinary.*

As Phil pulled into the parking stall Jewell had cracked the passenger side rear door open and waited. Shortly after Phil had left the car he first heard and then saw the Cad drive behind their car and turn into the parking stall next to their car on the driver's side.

As the hunters were talking between them Jewell slipped out the back door of Phil's car and slid out and behind the car next to his door. Moving low he slipped around behind that car and the one next to it and then stood up, keeping his back to the Cad, walked to the end of the porch and sat down on a bench. Both his guns were in his hands and shoved down between his legs.

The Cad parked in the spot next to Phil' car and the passenger got out and headed for the gallery door. He had not seen the person slipping out of the car next to them as they parked. On his way he walked over by Phil's car and looked inside. Phil expected a hail of bullets to come out of his car just about now, but nothing. Now he was really confused. The guy turned and started for the shop door.

Phil walked over to the counter and picked up one of the gallery brochures and then moved over to a wall of paintings. He had noticed one that was right down his alley when he first came in. He concentrated on the paintings and tried not to be too interested in the man coming through the door.

The man walked up beside him and stared at the paintings on the wall, kind of like he knew what he was looking at. Phil could tell the guy had no idea what a good piece of art was let alone knowing if it was oil or water color. Phil was sure that the guy knew who he was and that this was going to take hours before something finally happened.

The Man was scoping the shop out to try and determine who else was in the place and while doing that he kind of slid over close to Phil. He leaned over and close to Phil's ear. "Hey, you live in this area?"

Phil almost jumped; damn he knew the guy was there yet when he spoke to Phil he jumps. Phil looked at the man like he was some kind of an idiot. "No sir I don't."

The Man kept his voice low and leaned in toward Phil. "I saw you up around Newport at a restaurant, didn't I?" The guy kept his voice low, but even at that it was full of threat and intimidation. It was the kind of voice that caused you to squirm all over inside.

Phil's mind was going in every direction all at once he knew he had to answer, so he turned toward the man and said. "Well, yes you could have, I was up there yesterday."

The Man was still looking around and still leaning in toward Phil and continued to ask questions. "You're from Washington, aren't you?"

Phil managed to keep his cool and again turned and answered the question truthfully. "Why yes I am, Everett to be exact."

Phil then asked. "Is there a problem? Is there something I can help you with? Do I need to apologize for my poor driving demonstration a few minutes ago?"

The Man acted as if Phil had said nothing and just kept pushing as if he hadn't heard a word Phil said. "Did you come down from Everett on Interstate 5?

Phil turned toward the man and in an irritated voice said. "Yes sir, I did. I then turned west at Salem and came over to the coast highway. I take my vacation every year in Long Beach, California. There are a number of favorite places that I like to stop at when I come this way and this is one of them."

Just then the owner of the shop walked up and managed to squeeze in between Phil and The Man. The Owner knew Phil well and knew his schedule well. "Hi Phil, have you spotted anything you like so far?"

Phil took his attention away from the man "Oh, high Steve. Yes, I was looking at this one here, would you set it aside for me so that I can pick it up on my way back through."

The Owner smiled and reached up and took the painting down. "Sure, it'll be in the back and I'll see that it's wrapped and ready for you. The usual three weeks?"

Phil was thankful that the owner was a friend and knew him well. "That's right."

Steve, the owner, excused himself to the stranger as he took the painting off the wall and carried it away.

Then the guy asked. "Hey when I saw you making that turn in front of me, I noticed that you had Washington plates and as we passed you my buddy suggested that I check with you to see if you know of any really great restaurants south of here?" That was one hell of a lame excuse for coming in the shop after him, but Phil let it slide.

Phil could feel that he had finally satisfied the man and then said. "Well yes, I do. Just south of Crescent City is one of the best seafood restaurants in this part of the country. I stop in there at least once on my way south or when coming back. Just watch for the Pirates Hide Away Restaurant."

The Man offered his hand and said, "OK, thanks."

The Man turned and walked out the door. It took Phil several minutes to regain his composure as he walked over to the window and watched the Cad pull out of the lot and head south. Steve then walked up and handed him the receipt for the painting and Phil paid him and left.

When he got to his car he looked in and there was Jewell. How the hell did that guy miss him anyway, he's sitting right there where Phil had left him. Phil got into the car and just sat there.

Jewell came up over the seat and asked. "Phil, you, all right?" At the same time, he put his hand on Phil's shoulder.

Phil was still recovering. "Yeah, one of those guys followed me into the gallery and asked me a bunch of questions. They had seen the Washington State license plate on my car.

"Jewell, that passenger walked over by the car and looked in. I expected one hell of a gun fight, but he just walked away, what the hell happened."

Jewell told him. "I got out of the car as soon as you walked away and moved down by that bench and sat down on it with my back to your car.

Jewell sat there thinking for a few minutes. "What did you tell him?"

Phil turned and looked back at Jewel. "I told him the truth. I was heading for Long Beach like I do every year and this place, was one place I stopped off at every time I pass through. The owner Steve walked up then and I bought a painting and the guy left. They went south on the highway."

Jewell was still thinking and trying to determine what was happening and whether they were in the clear. "Do you think he was suspicious?"

Phil thought for a minute and then said. "At first, yes, but after talking to me I think he was satisfied that I was not involved with you. At least I hope they're satisfied."

Jewell sat back and laid his head on the back of the seat. "All right let's get out of here and head for California."

They pulled out of the lot and headed south again. Ten miles later they were running a part of 101 that was inland from the ocean. Traffic was light and it was getting into late afternoon. As they were going around a curve Phil looked in the rear-view mirror and there, they were three cars behind them.

"Get down!" Phil told Jewell. "They're back behind us, three cars back. Damn it anyway, how did they figure this one out?"

Jewell ducked down. "Yeah, they have us." Jewell had already gone into over drive and was preparing for what was to come. His system went into high gear and he prepared his mind and body for the gun fight that was coming. Two against one and an unarmed person present to protect. That's about right. No problem.

Phil could not understand what was going on and could not believe that they had them picked. "How did they know? How the hell did they figure this one out?"

Jewell had pulled both guns out and was getting ready for a minute of high-octane action. "Phil their predators and they can smell their prey when it's close by. They had us the moment they saw you back there at the left turn. They confirmed that when that guy came into the shop and talked to you. Don't worry about it, it had to come. It was just a matter of time."

Just then they passed a state police car parked along the road. Phil was watching when he saw the Cad pull over behind the patrol car. They pulled right up behind the patrol car and just then the patrol car's overhead lights went on.

Phil was watching the Cad as the driver was getting out of the car Phil turned to Jewell, "Jewell, their stopping behind that patrol car."

That caught Jewell by surprise. "What?"

Phil was trying to keep an eye ahead of them and watching the black Cad through the mirror "Yeah, they're pulling up behind the patrol car."

As they stopped behind the patrol car the officer turned his overhead lights on and got out of the patrol car. Phil could see the driver run to the officer and point in the direction of his car. He then rounded a curve and lost sight of them.

Jewell had to think fast, something bad was about to happen. "Just keep going and watch behind us, tell me what is going on with them."

A few minutes later Phil saw the patrol car coming around the curve behind them with its emergency lights on.

Phil checked in front of him and then yelled. "Jewell, that patrol car is coming up on us and is stopping us."

Jewell knew they had to get off the main highway and told Phil. "Take the next left turn."

Almost at that moment a secondary road came up and Phil made the turn and continued down the road. As it turned out there were no residences in that area. If they had picked this road on purpose, they could have done no better.

The patrol car came to the road and made the turn with the Cad right behind it. Both accelerated and came up behind Phil and then settled in to make the stop.

Jewell's mind was going full bore by this time. "All right now find a wide spot in the road and pull over. Keep half the car on the road so I have room on this side of the car. When you get stopped, get down as low as you can."

Phil's car had a center console and so he would have to slide down under the steering wheel. It was then that he spotted a wide area about a hundred yards long.

Jewell was telling Phil. "Find a spot and pull over now." His voice was full of drive and authority with an edge of menace to it.

Jewell had shifted in to the fight mode and was ready for total war. He had been there before and knew full well that people were going to die in the next thirty seconds. The problem was that he did not know who and how many. All he knew that none of the dead would be him or Phil.

Phil pulled onto the wide spot and brought the Ford to a stop as the patrol car came up behind him. The Cad came around the patrol car and swung in front of the Ford and about three car length ahead.

Phil called back to Jewell. "Jewell, the Cad parked in front of us, blocking us."

Jewell had his Glocks out and was ready for action. "All right, just stay down."

Jewell started to open the rear passenger door and got ready to swing out low and around the bottom of the door. The officer had left his unit and was walking up to the driver's door. He was just to the rear bumper when the driver and passenger in Cad

138

came out guns in hand. The driver went straight at the officer and opened up on him. He didn't have a chance. He had done what they wanted him to do and now he was expendable.

Jewell at the same time was swinging out of the back seat of the Ford and bringing the passenger of the Cad into his sights. Both the driver and Jewell opened up at the same time. Jewell's first round hit the passenger in the upper groin area, the shock of the round slammed through his body bringing him to a stop. That caused him to bend over, almost falling down and opening him up for the next shot. The second round hit in the neck. It went right through his spine. He dropped his gun and started to crumble. He was going down when the third round hit him in the right eye he was dead before he hit the ground.

Jewell swung up and around and centered in on the driver as he was coming around toward Jewell. Jewell's first round hit him in the upper arm and passed through and then into his body in the armpit area. That round passed almost armpit to armpit coming out just below his shoulder blade. Jewell's second round hit him in the lower left jaw and exited his right cheek. The shock of the two

139

rounds immobilized the gunman. He tried to recover but was not fast enough the third round hit him just above and forward of the left ear, in the temple area. He was already going down.

The whole thing lasted maybe six seconds. It all started with the officer being hit first and he was dead before he hit the ground. The other two followed in quick succession. After the initial battle was over Jewell walked over to the passenger and put another round through his head. Then over to the driver and did the same. He turned to Phil, yelling at him. "Open the trunk and get our luggage and throw them in the back seat of the Cad. I'll drive. Forget everything else."

Jewell was already moving around the back of the Cad and heading for the driver door. He was still operating at full speed. He knew that other cars could come along at any time, either another innocent or another patrol car. They had to get moving and moving now.

Phil had driven himself down under the steering wheel and was having trouble getting out from under it. He reached up and opened the door and then rolled backward out of the car and onto the ground. The first thing he saw was the dead gunman. He was lying on his stomach with his arms under him. His head was resting on his chin and looking right at Phil. It was the damnedest thing he had ever seen. He got up and reached into the car and pulled the keys and turned to walk back to the trunk. He was shaking, but the shock had not set in yet.

As he turned, he saw the officer lying on his side half way behind the back of the Ford. He felt sick, but managed to control himself. He stepped around the officer and got the trunk open and pulled the bags out of it. He was moving as fast as he could, but Jewell was yelling at him to hurry it up.

Jewell was pumped full of adrenaline and straining to see if anyone else was coming. "We got to get going now!"

Phil got to the Cad and dumped the bags in the back seat and jumped into the passenger's seat just as Jewell started the car.

They pulled away from the scene checking to see if any other cars were in the area. There were none. He turned on to the first road he came to and continued driving. At the next road he turned right and that took them back to 101, south toward California.

Jewell's entire system was operating as the hit-man that he was. "We have to get clear of this area as soon as possible. Those guys did not make this move without advising someone about where they were at and what they were about to do. Things have just gone from bad to worse.

"They killed a cop just to get at us and that means they will kill anyone and everyone they have to in order to put me down. Phil, your life has now become worthless."

As they traveled south two patrol cars came by them going north with their emergency lights going.

Jewell looked over at Phil "You all right, Phil, you, all right?"

Phil was still thinking about the officer and the price he had paid. "Yeah, what the hell just happened? That cop, why him?"

Jewell explained to Phil what the strategy of the killers was. "He was the tool they used to get us to stop. He was dead the minute they pulled in behind him. Phil, we have to get rid of this Cad as soon as we can. Once we're across the border we will work on doing that."

Phil's mind was numb from the event and was finding it hard to function, "How are we going to get another car." For the first time Phil was the passenger and he was having a hard time trying to determine what to do with his hands, he had to do something, there had to be a way to use his hands while sitting there. His mind was still trying to deal with what had just happened, in less than ten seconds he had seen three men die and now he was running from both the mob and police.

Jewell had two problems one being Phil and his first experience in a gun battle. He could see both hands shaking as he drove the Cad toward California. Phil was a good guy, but he was not accustomed to this kind of action. The sight of all that blood and death, including that cop, made Phil a bomb looking for a place blow. All he needed was one more surprise event and he would blow and that would doom the two of them. He had a choice either eliminate Phil or work him through this thing. He couldn't eliminate him.

Jewell was thinking way ahead of Phil and their situation and his second problem, finding another car. The Cad would only work for them for a short time, less than twenty-four hours, and then it would become a huge target rolling down the road. Jewell then said to Phil. "We need to get rid of this car as soon as possible. We'll buy one at a local lot or out of the classified ads. I prefer the classified."

Phil finally started to think again and asked, "Where we going to dump the car?"

Jewell had already made that determination and explained to Phil. "The biggest parking lot we can find that has a lot of activity. We'll get a paper and check the ads and then call them and see if they will bring the car to the parking lot so we can buy it."

Phil still did not know what was happening. "How do we do that?"

Jewell continued to explain their actions. "Our car broke down and we need transportation. We'll meet them in the store and make the deal. The key is to make it appear to be as safe as it can be. No haggling on this one. If we get someone to come, we'll pay and get the hell out of there."

Finally, they crossed the border and were just a short distance to Crescent City. It was just sixteen miles from the border. Phil had turned the radio on to see if they could find anything out about the event, there was nothing.

Phil was still struggling to understand. He asked. "What kind of store do we want? I'm not sure we'll find the store we need."

Jewell explained in a slow and

controlled manner. "We need one of the big box stores, not a grocery store. You know a Home Depot or something like that. We want the place with the most activity, the more cars in the parking lot the better."

Sure, enough as they entered the town there was the store they needed and its lot was almost full. Jewell found a spot way out in the farthest reaches of the parking lot. They took their things from the car and threw the keys in the trunk and then locked it up.

They walked into the store with their suitcases and found a paper and started going through the ads. Phil wasn't too sure he wanted to be standing around in some store waiting for someone to bring them a car, but he had no alternative other than to just stick with Jewell.

Jewell was busy scanning the local car ads in the newspaper when he found what he wanted. If he could get the owner to bring that car to them, he and Phil would be back on the road within minutes of the car's arrival. The car that he found would meet their every need. It was fast and it was a road car and right now that was what they needed. The ad read, 2002 Ford Mustang dark blue and in perfect condition, price thirty thousand dollars.

The price seemed a little steep to Jewell, but the car was what they needed and right now he had little choice. He needed to talk to the owner and see the car before he was going to spend that kind of money. But, on the other hand, he had little time and few options, so thirty thousand didn't seem to be that much considering the situation.

Phil called the number and a man answered. He told the man his problem and where they were at. The man at first was reluctant to come, but after talking a few minutes he decided he would come. He said that he wanted to pick up a friend on the way. Phil told him that would be just fine with them. He told them where in the store they were and then hung up.

Forty minutes later two men walked through the door. One was carrying some papers. Phil waved to them. Both walked up and everyone introduced themselves. Jewell and Phil used aliases. After a few minutes of small talk, the owner of the car took Jewell outside to look the car over.

As Jewell walked up to the car he almost froze in his tracks. Jewell knew they had hit pay dirt, "How much?" He asked. He knew that the ad had said thirty thousand, but by the looks of this rig that was a bargain price. The car had to be worth a whole lot more than what they were asking for it.

The seller said without hesitation. "Thirty." He continued. "I need the money as soon as I can get it and so I have to sell her a little short of what she is really worth.

Jewell couldn't help it; this was something he had not expected and as he listened to the seller, he knew the guy was in real need of the cash. That put Jewell in the most enviable position and that meant that he had to haggle, "How about twenty-five thousand cash?"

The guy stood there looking at him, "For real?" He was not sure if he even heard Jewell right. He was looking at his car and mulling over what Jewell had offered. Jewell could see that this guy was having one hell of a hard time and that the need to sell was over shadowing his common sense.

Jewell needed to add some more punch to his offer and pulled a wad of money out of his pocket, "Cold cash, here and now."

The guy stood there looking at the car, he was in a real tight spot and there was a huge fight going on in his head over the need to sell and the lack of people interested in buying a car of this type. He then turned to Jewell and asked, "twenty-five thousand cash?"

Jewell showed him the money. "Yeah, right here, right now."

He looked back at the car and then back to Jewell. "It's yours."

The car, it was a 2002 Mustang Saleen S281 Extreme, dark blue in color and in mint condition. Jewell liked what he saw. He knew that was just the car for what was to come, so why not go out in style. They shook hands and then turned and walked away from the car.

They returned to the others and made the deal. Jewell paid him counting out twenty-five thousand dollars into his hand in cash, the friend standing there watched and as Jewell counted the friend's mouth dropped that much more open.

With the cash paid the owner signed the car over to Jewell and they shook hands again. As the men left, the seller turned to Jewell and asked about their broken-down car. "You guys going to come back for the other car? If not, maybe we could work out a deal to take it off your hands?"

Jewell thanked them and then told them. "We will be coming back through here in a couple of weeks and will pick it up at that time and take it back home with us."

They nodded and left. Jewell and Phil took their suitcases, and went out to the Mustang, and loaded them into the trunk. They left the lot and headed south. They decided to drive all night and get as much distance between them and the gun fight as they could. Besides Jewell needed to get some practice in driving this rig, it was a road car and he needed to gain a feel for it.

Phil was just beginning to understand the magnitude of what had happened that evening. He had been involved in the death of three men and was now in so deep he couldn't figure a way out of it. No, his best bet was to stick with Jewell, at least he knew what he was doing and if left alone Phil probably would have been in jail before morning.

Phil looked over at Jewell and said. "That's fifteen."

Jewell looked at him and just started to laugh. Phil found himself starting to laugh as well and they both let it all out. About thirty minutes later they came by an all-night restaurant and pulled in to get something to eat.

As they sat there Phil asked Jewell. "What's next?"

Jewell looked at him. "Phil this is like a chess game. They make a move and we make a move. They surely reported in that they had located me and where and with who and what we were driving. Others are moving into the area and are looking for us right now. The fact that we changed cars will be in our favor. The problem is that they will figure that out real fast, if they haven't already.

"Right now, we're doing well. They had us checked and we turned that around and now have them checked. Right now, we're in a tight spot being in this area. There are not many places to go, so when we're finished here, we're going to head east back to the Interstate 5 area. I want to run secondary roads from now on, staying off the Interstates."

Phil realized that Jewell was thinking way ahead of him, "All right with me. Right now, I'm starving and ready to have a big meal."

Jewell nodded, "Me too."

Phil was still trying to understand. "Jewell, do you think we'll be able to checkmate them?"

They sat there silently eating as Jewell got his thoughts together. He then looked up at Phil and nodded. "Yes, I think we have a good chance to do just that. We are now going to change the rules of the game and that will leave them in a state of confusion and indecision. In time they will figure it out and then shift into that arena and come after us again. I would say that we have maybe a day and a half to two days before they get it.

"In that time, we will need to develop a plan of action and set it in motion. I would guess that by the time we get that done they will be breathing down our necks again. What they don't know is just what I'm about to do and by the time they figure that out, it's going to be too late."

As Phil looked at Jewell, he could see the cold calculating mind of a man with little or no feelings or compassion. He knew that this man was a perfect machine that was always thinking and keeping a running account of his actions and movements in this death game he was playing.

He was beginning to realize that he was in this man's jungle and he was at the mercy of all that crawled and crept through, in and around in it. He was out of his realm and he knew it. His only hope of surviving was to stick with Jewell and stick close.

He felt lost in this game and hoped that Jewell would eventually explain everything to him as it became necessary. It was like being invited to play a game you have never played before and everyone else has. When the first play is made, all you can do is stand there and wonder what the hell you were supposed to do.

Phil was depending on Jewell to tell him what and when to do his part. Did that sound right or was he just crazy as hell. He didn't like it one bit, but he had little choice at this time. It was Jewell's game and he had to follow Jewell's lead. He just hoped that somewhere down the road he would be free again to live his own life. We'll see.

Chapter Six

DARKNESS IS SAFER

From the restaurant they headed back north on 101 and then took highway 11 which tied into California State Route 199 going east. This route took them back to the Oregon border and to Grants Pass. They then got onto old Highway 99E also called the Rogue River Highway and turned south again. By this time, it was mid-morning and they found a motel they could get into.

Their best bet was to hole up for the day and travel at night. By staying with the secondary roads and traveling only at night they would be at an advantage over their hunters. What Phil failed to recognize was the fact that Jewell was a hunter as well. That he was not just running, but was maneuvering and trying to put them into the most advantageous position possible. He was in his element and there were few who could match him.

Now they had both the mob and the police hunting them after the shootout. They knew that the police would, in time figure out what actually happened, but for the time being they had to run on the basis that both the mob and police were after them. That meant that as they drove, they stayed with the traffic. No high-speed runs and no erratic driving, do nothing that will attract anyone's attention. Just two guys heading south.

It was nine that evening when they left the motel and headed south. While driving Jewell started talking about where they were going. "Phil, I know you want to go to Long Beach, but the further south we go the greater the probability that they will catch up with us. By now they know L.A. is our probable target. Maybe we need to head east, say Nevada."

Phil sat there trying to follow Jewell's train of thought. His vacation had, for all intent and purposes, been completely wiped out. He thought about Jewell's comment and then looked over at him. "Yeah, I think you're right. If we keep pressing south, we're going to drive right into them. What are your plans for heading toward Nevada?"

Jewell was already working that out in his mind, he had been looking at a map back at the motel and had a route worked out. "Just south of here is Shasta, we can take highway 89 east to Susanville and then from there on into Nevada to Reno. We can do it by morning and then hole up there and decide our next move."

It was agreed and they swung over and got on to Interstate 5 and headed south. They felt that they could make better time while running at night. Their plan was to turn east at Shasta on to 89 and then stop in McCloud for something to eat. Then it would be on to Reno or Sparks whichever they wanted when they got there.

It was then that Jewell asked Phil. "Phil, are you ready to carry a gun?" Jewell needed a backup and Phil was the only one around that could do that, but first, Jewell had to get Phil to carry and use a gun. It was a gamble and one that would be the key to all his plans. This was the time to ask the question, the only problem was what Phil's response would be.

Phil had already been thinking about it and was still a little apprehensive about the idea. "Jewell, back at the fight if I had a gun, I wouldn't have known what to do. I have never had to use one nor have I ever been in a fight of any kind let alone a gun battle. I just don't know if I would be a help or a detriment. Guns have never been a part of my life and are just something I see in the movies and on television, but to hold one and pull the trigger, I'm not sure of at all.

"I have no idea if I could carry out any kind of a plan involving the use of a gun and having to target another human being. I don't think I'm a coward, but I also don't think I could really do that. I need time to think." He sat there a few minutes trying to work his way around what Jewell had asked him. "I just don't know right now, but I also know I need to deal with it."

Jewell was listening intently to Phil trying to measure him and decide if he could do it under the right circumstances. "I understand Phil. No, I'm talking more in the line of last resort, if I'm taken down and you're left alone. It would at least give you a fighting chance to make it. You may not feel that you could fire a gun, let alone fire it at someone, but under the right circumstances I can assure you that you could and would."

Phil hadn't thought about that and now realizes Jewell was right. "I see what you mean. Well, let me think on that point of view for a few. I need to do some soul searching before I jump in to it." Phil's mind was racing ahead and trying to deal with the specter of carrying a weapon and then having to use it. Yet he knew, based on what had happened so far, he would certainly be involved in additional situations that would be a threat to his life, to Jewell's life, and the necessity for him to step up and take the jump.

Jewell nodded his head, but warned him that they did not have a lot of time for contemplation. "Phil, I understand. I just want you to know if you want, I have a gun here that would be perfect for you and is easy to learn to use. Think about it and if the answer is yes, when we get to a motel, I'll work you through it."

Phil was looking at Jewell and wondering just how he had gotten involved in this thing in the first place. Yes, Mom was right. It then came to his mind that Jewell was right, he was right on the button about Phil's chances of survival without having some means of defending himself. With that he said. "All right, I'll do it."

Jewell nodded his head and said nothing. He knew Phil had just made one of the biggest decisions in his life and what was to come would be even more traumatic.

They made it on into Susanville and then on down to Reno. They found a motel off the main gut and checked in. When they got to their room Phil sat down and looked at Jewell. Phil had come to a determination and was ready to talk. "Jewell, I've been thinking."

By the mannerism in Phil's voice Jewell knew something was coming and focused on Phil, "What about?"

Phil then started to work his way through the morass of the past few days. "Well, we're into this thing up to our necks. We have no one working for our welfare and no one available to keep us informed as to what is going on."

Jewell was thinking, this sure as hell isn't about a gun. "Yes, I agree."

Phil then leaned toward Jewell. "What would you think if we called my attorney and brought him on board?" Phil said in an almost apologetic tone.

Jewell looked a little puzzled, he didn't like dealing with attorneys, cops, judges, or anyone remotely tied to the law. It was not something he really cared to think about, but it occurred to him that somewhere along the line they may well find themselves in a situation that would require it. Jewell asked. "Like what could he do?"

Phil got down to business and continued. "We could fill him in on what has been going on and the position we're in. I think we need someone on our side that could be an advocate for us in the event this thing does get into a court. Besides that, we will have our own record of what took place and it will be held by an impartial third party."

Jewell was starting to see the angle Phil was coming from. "All right, say we do, how are we going to contact him?"

Phil continued. "Jewell, I doubt that the mob knows I have an attorney and who he is. I doubt that the police know that much. We would call him from here and set up a computer link or e-mail exchange and work everything that way. I'm sure they don't have my attorney bugged so one call would be safe.

"Once past that point then we can get a laptop and I can set up an encrypted link with him and we can do everything via computer and there will be a permanent record of it as well."

Jewell sat there a few minutes. He understood what Phil was saying and could see the value in it. As he mulled Phil's idea over in his head he started to nod. "I think you have something there. Who's your attorney?"

Phil was not clearly excited about the prospects of bringing his attorney on board. "His name is David Spalding and his office is in Everett. He's a good attorney and has been in the business twenty years or more. He has good experience and I trust him."

Jewell's mind was charging off ahead of Phil and trying to decide the long-range advantage of Phil's idea before he jumped. "When do you want to do this?"

Phil shrugged his shoulders. "Now, we're not going anywhere right now, so this would be a good time to start."

Jewell still had reservations. "Wait, you said we would use computers?"

"Right." Phil replied.

Jewell pointed out one clear and present issue. "Phil, we don't have one."

Phil already knew what they needed and where to get it. "I know, but we will buy one. There is a mall across the street I'll just go over there and buy a good laptop and bring it back and we're ready to go."

The lights went on for Jewell and he leaned back and raised both hands. "Hey, I forgot you're a computer geek. I think you're on to something. You want to go by yourself?"

Phil was clearly into this thing and was more than ready to go. "Yes, I think that would be best, don't you?" Then he stopped and looked at Jewell. "Jewell, I'm not going to run."

Jewell looked at him. "Yeah, I know, but it's just me, I find it hard to trust anyone other than myself. If I screw up, I have no one else to blame. It's just me and I can't help it, sorry."

Phil told Jewell he would need about twenty-five hundred to get the laptop and support software and hardware he would need. Jewell gave him four thousand and Phil headed for the mall.

Jewell had taken a huge calculated risk in giving Phil the money and letting him go on his own. As he thought about it, he remembered the restaurant when he took to the beach and Phil met him down the road. Or the motels, when Phil let him off at one and then went to another and still showed up the next morning. No, he was sure that he had a trusted friend and partner in Phil. He would be back.

Meanwhile, Jewell sat back and started to think on his next move and direction of travel. He had not related to Phil what his overall plan was and when he did, he wanted it all ready to go. Jewell was not the prey type of person. He was a predator and everything he did and thought was from that point of view. Up till now he had been the prey and was running and reacting to the hunter, but now he felt it was time to reverse the roles and that would put him in his comfort zone, if being a hired killer had a comfort zone.

As he went over the maps, he had picked up he was formulating a plan of attack. It was time that he stopped running and started attacking. That was his mode of operation. As a predator he was conditioned to seek out and attack, to take the action to the other side and hit them hard and often. He was now shifting and he had his prey targeted and was ready to seek it out and kill.

An hour later Phil was knocking on the motel room door. Jewell opened the door and Phil came in arms loaded.

Jewell couldn't believe the load of hardware. "Gees man, you buy out the whole place?"

"Just about, but I got everything we'll need for this job." Phil replied.

Phil immediately got to work setting the laptop up. In forty minutes, he was on line and ready to contact his attorney.

Jewell then suggested they go get breakfast and then do the attorney thing after that. An hour later they were back in the room and Phil picked up the phone and made the call. When the secretary of his attorney answered he told her who he was. He listened for any odd reactions from her, but got none.

"Oh, good morning, Mister Morles."

Phil's mind was racing and he all most forgot the secretary's name. "Hi Ginny, is David available?"

Ginny had been working for her boss a number of years and clearly knew who he would accept calls from and those he would not. "Yes, he is Mr. Morles, just a moment please."

Seconds later I answered the phone,

"Morning Phil how's it going?"

Phil paused a minute to gather his thoughts. This was not going to be easy and he felt a little guilty dropping something like this on David out of the blue. "David, I'll know that after we talk." The cue line had been given and now Phil had to wait to see if I caught on and wanted to continue.

I knew with those words that something was in the wind. I have been in this business too long to not know when one of my clients was under pressure and as soon as Phil spoke, I knew. "Phil what's up?"

I had moved into my official mode and made ready for what was to follow, whatever it was. "Phil, is this an attorney to client situation?"

Phil knew he could not beat around the bush with me and gave it to me straight. "Yes, David it is and it's a big one."

I geared up for an in-your-face situation. The edge in Phil's voice told me that this was not the normal civil type issue, Phil was in trouble and I would need all my experience to deal with Phil's needs. "How big?" I asked.

Phil decided not to pull any punches he had to give me the heavy side of the situation up front. He knew that what he had to say would determine whether I would stay his attorney or back out and advise Phil to seek other help. "My life David, just my life."

There was a long pause.

I reached over and opened my desk drawer. "Do I need to record this?"

Phil knew now that the situation was serious and this was now a full-blown client to attorney situation. "I think you should David, I don't want to go through this thing all over again."

I took a deep breath and prepared myself for what was coming. I have known Phil for many years and knew that he was not one to go out and jump into trouble. If Phil was calling about something serious, then it was serious and involved. "All right, give me a minute."

Two minutes later there was a beep on the line and I came back on.

I took another deep breath. "We're recording now Phil. Fill me in."

Phil went into the whole thing from the time he left home on vacation this past Saturday to the present. There was a long pause on the line as he worked to organize his thoughts. It was one of those pauses you experience when someone is applying every ounce of energy, they have to the mental issue that they were facing at that moment in time. I was sure Phil was wondering if I was weighing all the odds and issues carefully.

For a minute there Phil had thought that I had hung up on him, "David you there?"

I was still thinking and knew the silence could be a problem, I came back on. "Yes Phil, I'm here."

Phil could tell that I was not happy with what he had just told him. He had a real bad feeling about this whole thing now and wished he had not called. "Sorry for all this David."

I was busy getting myself set up and into high gear to continue on with Phil. I had known Phil for years and knew full well that when Phil needed help, he really needed it. Beside Phil had never brought this serious an issue to me before.

I was sure the extenuating circumstances were exceptional. "Phil that's what I'm here for. I don't get many calls like this, so you have to understand that I have to get myself straight and in the lawyer mode.

I paused. "Is Mister Scarpone there now?" I asked.

Phil looked at Jewell and then said. "Yes, he is and he's listening in."

I then turned my attention to Jewell. "Mister Scarpone?"

Jewell never found it easy to speak to an attorney, any attorney, whether his own or one for the government. He hated placing his fate in someone else hands, "Yes, sir."

I had to get Jewell to agree to have me represent him as well as Phil. "Would you concur with what Phil has said so far?"

Jewell took a deep breath. "Yes, sir I do."

I then started to dig deeper into the relationship between the two of them. "Now, will you fill me in on what brought Phil to this point, and start from when you first met him?"

Jewell filled me in with every bit of information about what happened and how he ended up at the rest stop and in contacting Phil. When he finished there was another long pause on the other end.

I now had to address the needs of my client. "Phil, do you want to get out from under this situation and away from Mister Scarpone."

That was the big question and it was

one that Phil and Jewell had to face. This was it, Phil had to make that final and possibly fatal decision then and there, he had no way around it. Phil looked at Jewel and started to answer my question. "David, we both wish that was possible, but right now it's not. No matter what I do, I am marked. I am currently safer staying with Jewell than going it alone."

Now I had to determine just what Phil's situation was. Though both were basically my clients now, Phil was still my primary client. I then asked. "You sure your targeted?"

Phil got directly with me and told it just like it was. He didn't pull any punches, leaving nothing out. "David, they killed that cop just to get at us. Do you understand that, they killed that poor SOB because they wanted to get at the two of us? They wanted us so bad they killed that officer without a second thought. That no good asshole gunned that officer down without giving any warning or without any sense of guilt, when that guy died, I had no feelings for him at all, he got what he deserved."

He had my attention at that point. This was the proverbial life and death situation. "Right, I understand that Phil."

Still Phil pushed his feeling home to

me. I knew they were not going to be able to keep this phone thing up for very long and I told Phil that. They needed to move on to the next phase of whatever Phil was planning.

Phil was expecting that comment to come and was ready for him. "I know that David, so I have bought a laptop and software so that we can set up a link between us, I will encrypt it and then carry on the bulk of our activity that way. We can also set up a video link so that we can see one another from time to time."

I was impressed with the way Phil and Jewell were setting this whole thing up. They were thinking and holding nothing back and that was important to an attorney. "That sounds good. When do you want to do it?"

"I can do it right now David."

"All right. What do you need?"

Phil then told me what he needed from me to set up the link between us. "Give me your e-mail address and your messenger address and I'll set it up right now."

Phil went to work making the internet link and implementing the encryption system. "David, do you have a camera with your computer."

"Yes, I do."

Phil continued his work on the link up. "All right then now give me about ten minutes and I'll make internet contact with you and we'll be set."

I agreed and ended the telephone contact, sat back to wait for Phil to come back to me on the internet. "All right, I'll stand by until I receive your contact Phil."

Ten minutes later Phil hit the enter key and the linkup took place. When I came back to Phil, he told me to stand by that he was going to tie us together and then encrypt our connection. That was done successfully and we were ready to start.

Phil advised me as to what they would be doing. "David, we are going to sit down and layout what our plans are going to be for the next two days. We'll then get back to you and let you know the schedule. In addition, as you think of needs, just send them to us and we'll address them from here."

"That's good for me Phil. Talk later." I hit the disconnect key and sat back in my chair. That was probably one of the most intense situations I had ever been in during my twenty plus years in the business. I called my secretary in and for the next hour we prepared the files and records for whatever came in from Phil and Jewell. I would need all my skill and patience while dealing with this mess I did not like it at all, but that was what I was paid for.

They disconnected and Phil turned to Jewell. "All right what are our plans?"

Jewell sat back and looked at Phil. "That my dear Phil is going to straighten your hair out."

By this time Phil had come to expect just about anything out of Jewell. "What are you talking about?"

The room fell quiet as they both sat there thinking about what tomorrow may or may not bring. They had just entered into a whole new phase in their relationship and it would bring an even greater degree of danger to their lives. Phil didn't know it, but Jewell was ready to take the initiative and carry the fight to those who were after them.

Jewell began to elaborate on his ideas. "Well, while you were gone, I had a chance to sit back and do some thinking. So far all I've done is run. Once I met you it was the same except this time you were running as well. Look, we can only run for so long and then they, someone, is going to find us and when they do it will be under their conditions and location of choice. I don't like that, and it means sure death to both of us."

Phil knew that the gun thing would be coming up again somewhere in this conversation and at the same time knew that Jewell was right. After all, he knew these people and how they thought. "Jewell, what are you proposing?"

Jewell placed both hands on the table and leaned toward Phil. "Phil, I want to go on the offensive."

That was a new one for Phil and all he could do was repeat what Jewell had said, "On the offense?"

Jewell nodded his head. "Yeah, I want to go right at old man Benito and take the fight right to him. I'm done running from him and I'm now going to start running at him."

Have you ever had that feeling that someone just pushed a button and all hell was about to cut lose, well Phil did just then and he could hardly believe what was just said. "Jewell, I don't know if I like that idea. No, I'm sure I don't like it."

Jewell waved his right hand. "Just hear me out all right. Here is what I would like to do." He started presenting a plan so outrageous and daring that Phil had little

172

doubt neither one of them could possibly come out of it alive.

Jewell continued. "Instead of running all over the country reacting to their moves and actions, I want to plan a trip back to where it all started."

Phil's eyes were starting to get bigger and tear up. "You mean Tinley Park?"

Jewell was determined that he had the right idea and he pressed it. "Right, Tinley Park, except that we will probably end up in the southwest side of Chicago, far enough away to be safe but close enough to get the job done."

Crap this is getting out of hand, thought Phil. "And then what?"

Jewell looked Phil straight in the eyes. "Then we target Benito."

Phil looked back and in a low almost deadly voice. "We target Benito?"

Jewell let the reaction of Phil's pass and confirmed that was what he said. "Yes, the old man."

Target, what the hell was he up to, thought Phil. "And, by target, what do you mean?"

Jewell put both hands palm down on the table top and looked at Phil. "Phil, I mean we kill the son-of-a-bitch."

Every good mystery movie has that moment, that dramatic pause, just before a major event in the plot takes place. Well, it was time for that pause right now. The two men sat there looking at one another. Neither moved nor did the expressions on their faces change, they just sat there looking at each other.

One was thinking this is getting more and more insane. The other, it's the only way out for us. If we don't, we're dead, period.

God, I wish I was someplace else right now, Phil thought. He finally sat back in his chair, but still looking straight at Jewell. "All right Jewell, let's hear it."

At that point Jewell started laying his plan out in detail for Phil. He was talking about traveling over one thousand six hundred miles from Reno to the Greater Chicago area. And that was as the crow flies. They would actually have to head that way in a zigzag pattern so as to avoid the police and mob while heading back.

Once there, the plan was to locate Benito and then kill him. He was the last of his family. Ben's death had left him all alone. His wife had passed on several years earlier and so he was basically living all alone. Yes, he had his organization, but that did not guarantee that they would go along with everything he wanted. The fact was that there was always someone looking for a way or means of deposing the family boss and taking his place. It was not an issue of loyalty; it was just business.

As Jewell laid out his plan Phil worked the computer, going in and using one of the global programs that are available to lay out the best route and then work their way to Benito's location.

They found his home and had a great aerial view of the compound. They determined that the compound was not the place to target. They needed to target him at his downtown business location or while he was in-route to or from there.

As the plan came together Phil became more aware of the fact that he knew this was the only way to get free of the threat of that man and hopefully survive. It was an audacious plan, but one that could work if they did their homework and applied their skills. Phil was learning more than he really wanted to know, but he also knew that if he did not know the plan and the process, he would be more of a detriment than a partner.

Phil finally looked at Jewell, cleared his throat and then said. "I think I'm going to need to learn how to handle that gun."

Jewell had been waiting for that commitment from Phil. He knew it had to come; the question was when. Finally, it had come. He then asked, "You sure?"

Phil didn't like it, but it appeared it was going to be necessary. "Look, Jewell, right now I'm going to die. If this plan is successful, I live. If it fails and I die trying, that's better than dying on my knees begging."

Jewell was impressed with this guy's attitude, taking into consideration that a few days back he was the geek of computers, now he was a man ready to fight for his life. Jewell sat there looking at him. "Yeah, I understand. I feel the same way myself."

Over the course of the next three days the two men completed their planning phase and Jewell put Phil through a firearms training session that included everything except actual firing the weapon. They did do a lot of dry firing though. Jewell wanted Phil to get to know the trigger pull of both guns and the methods in loading and ejecting the clips as he used them. By the end of the three days

Phil was proficient in his handling of the guns. All that was needed was time on a range or someplace where he could actually fire them.

On the morning of the fourth day Phil contacted me. He advised me that they would be leaving the Reno area, but made sure he said nothing about going after Benito. As long as I knew nothing about their plans, I was in the clear to advocate for them when the time comes.

It was then that Phil asked me about my fee. Phil knew that they needed to tie me down as their attorney and to insure the attorney and client relationship. "David, I know there is a cost here and we have decided to advance you a fee in the event that things happen and we can't get around to paying you. This way you will have the authorization to oversee our legal needs."

I did not like the sound of that, but understood what was going on. "Phil, that works fine for me. How much are we talking about?"

Phil looked at Jewell and Jewell nodded his head. "David, we want to forward to you fifty thousand as a retainer."

There was a long pause.

I was almost speechless when I heard that. "You have that much on hand?"

"Yes, we do and it was not stolen money."

I agreed and then told Phil what to do. "All right, here's my bank account number and bank."

Jewell advised that he uses the same bank so that would work just fine.

Phil then advised me of their next activity. "We'll be leaving here in about an hour and will make the deposit and then transfer the money to your account. When we clear the area, I'll notify you. We plan on contacting you once each day and letting you know how things are going. Now if we don't, please don't try to locate us. We will eventually contact you even if it's been a week, all right?

"We will have to stay loose and that means that if we need to move fast, we will not be able to complete our contacts with you. Don't let that worry you it's just the way things will be. If anything, real disastrous happens you'll know about it anyway."

I was curious about their destination, "Can I ask where you're going?"

Phil knew that I would ask but then

advised me. "David, we're going back to Chicago to clear this mess up. Hopefully we can do it without any loss of life."

I paused for a moment. "All right Phil, keep me posted and I'll start working on your legal issues here."

There are always some things that seem to never be finished and then it dawned on Phil, "One other thing David.

I was busying trying to determine my next move and automatically said. "What's that?"

Phil knew that things were going to be crazy for some time after they left Reno and he had forgotten about his job. "In two and a half weeks I am supposed to be back to work. I may not make it. I need you to notify my boss that I am in a situation and I may not get back on time. Basically, cover my ass for me David."

I made a note and advised Phil, "That I'll do Phil. Anything special you want me to tell them."

Phil stopped and waited a few to see if anything else popped up and nothing came. "Just that I'm in a bad way and you have no other information on it, but I will advise them as to when I can be back."

"Will do Phil." I replied.

An hour later they were on the road heading out of Reno. Jewell was driving and Phil was co-pilot. He had set up the laptop with a global tracking program. They did not want just a simple GPS, but wanted to track their location and Phil would have the ability to scan ahead and check the roads and routes out before they got there. That way they were totally free to alter and redirect their travel as needed.

Phil had put together a complete wireless satellite linked system. This way he was able to keep track of any and all local activities that would affect traffic movement or any other police activity that could interrupt their movements. As they moved Phil was continually scanning news, weather, and road condition sites and then selecting the best route through that area.

Jewell had his usual Glock Model 22's ready to go. Phil had two Glock Model 19"s, each one loaded with 15 rounds. This model was compact and an easier weapon for a new user to control. It shot the nine-millimeter round. That gave them a total of one hundred twenty rounds to start with, thirty rounds total for each gun. There were also four extra clips for both men, which gave them sixty more rounds each. Needless to say, they were loaded for bear and now the battle lines had been drawn.

Both men were running through their minds what they were feeling and if this was the right thing to do. Phil knew that if he wanted to have a life free of threat, he needed to carry this thing through. That time, way back a hundred years or so, when he was just a computer geek going south for his annual vacation was another time and another life. He was now a wholly new person, a man fighting for whatever was left of his time, his place, his life.

Jewell, though a hunter predator, had never been in this type situation before and he was redefining. He knew that every ounce of skill, knowledge, and courage he could dig up would have to come to the forefront now. There was no turning back, no reconsidering, no different plan. It was just this one issue, this one goal, this one choice.

Make no mistake about it, they were a team and they were dependent on one another. There was only one ending that was satisfactory to them and that was the death of Benito. He had to go. There was no other way around it. If the two of them wanted to live then he, Benito, had to die.

There was a shifting, a change taking place and it was one that would carry them the rest of the way to their target. They were moving from the hunted to the hunter. They were no longer the prey. They had now changed to the predator and there was only one purpose left in their lives. That was the finding and the killing of their prey, whether he knew he was the prey or not. In time he would know, by then it would be too late.

What had started out as a lonely battle for life way back then in Chicago and the killing of his friend Ben was now a new friend and a fight to live a life free of threat or attack. Jewell had come a long way and he had a long way to go. Phil would be the one unexplained element that came into his life and gave him the feeling that success was possible.

Chapter Seven

SNAKES IN THE DESERT

Heading out of Reno they got onto Interstate 80 and headed across Nevada to the Utah border, about three hundred sixty miles, as the crow flies and then another one hundred twelve miles to Salt Lake City. Their plan at the time was to hole up in Provo, just south of Salt Lake and continue east into Colorado to Denver. From there they would review how things were going and make a decision as to which direction to go.

About seventy miles east of Reno Jewell turned off on to a side road and headed out into the desert. Phil asks him where he was going and Jewell looked over at him.

"You've done a lot of learning and training with those guns, but as yet you haven't used them. So, we are going to get a few minutes of target practice before we go any further."

They drove maybe ten miles into the desert before Jewell pulled up and stopped. He turned the engine off and sat there a few minutes looking the area over and turned to Phil.

"I'm not interested in how good a shot you are; I just want to make sure you know how to handle the guns and work the mechanism. This is not about being a crack shot, it's about making them work when you want and need them to."

Jewell located an isolated spot with a small hill they could use as a backdrop. At first all he wanted was to see if Phil knew how to fire the weapon. He was clumsy at it the first time, damn near shot Jewell in the foot. After the fourth time he started to look like he had a handle on using a gun.

They had gone through five clips by this time and Phil was getting into a rhythm. He was not great, but he was familiar with the process and theory behind using a weapon proficiently during a battle. Whether he would be able to during an actual battle was yet to be seen. Jewell was sure he would have his hands full just overseeing Phil and trying to make sure he survived.

After the last round of shooting, Phil was picking up the spent clips and cleaning them up. Jewell watched him closely and noted a small tremble of his hands. He was satisfied that it was just a small tremble and not one that compromised his ability to hold and fire the weapon.

"How do you feel about that thing and the way it felt in your hands when firing it?" Jewell asked.

Phil looked at the guns and turned them over in his hand, "I guess they're all right. Haven't fired one before, but it felt good and I didn't have a problem holding them level and swinging them from target to target."

Jewell smiled, he would do all right, he thought. The fact is even the best and oldest of shooter could die when the first round is fired. It was kind of a crap shoot to say the least.

The fact was Phil looked to be a natural shooter. He automatically swung in on his target and held the weapons level during every move. Few people showed that ability right off the bat and that made Phil something of a miracle. Jewell knew that when involved in a firefight Phil would respond automatically and that was good from his position.

Once they were done with the target practice, their plan was to continue on to Salt Lake City. There they would turn south on Interstate 215 to Provo where they decided to hole up till the next day. At this point they had not seen or been observed by any law enforcement agency.

They got into the car and headed back toward I-80 and on to Salt Lake. They kept their heads and maintained a good speed that matched the traffic. That is, if there was any traffic out in the desert. Up till then Jewell had no feelings that anything was wrong. It wasn't until they were another thirty miles down the road when the gray Corvette came up behind them.

He had not been worried about it when he first saw it come into view. After all, they were in the desert and the road was straight as an arrow and some drivers took that opportunity to see just how fast they could go and it appeared that is just what this guy was doing.

It was when he pulled up behind them

and then stayed there that it started to dawn on him there could be a problem. There was no other traffic coming at them or running with them and this guy had come up on them at well over a hundred miles an hour and then slowed and fell in behind them and stayed there.

Jewell reached over and nudged Phil.

Phil looked over at Jewell and asked, "What do you need."

Jewell swept his eyes across all three review mirrors, "We've got company."

Jewell could feel Phil tighten up.

"Phil, relax and take it easy we're not in trouble yet, just get ready. This one guy is not going to be a problem it's the car full out there ahead of us that will be the problem.

"Now get that computer going and let me know how far it is to the next fuel or restaurant stop. Then I need you to find a cut off. A road that will go out into the desert and then double back to the main road, past that fuel or restaurant stop, got that."

"How the hell did they get on us so fast?" Phil asked.

"They have probably had every city within a thousand miles of the gunfight covered watching for us leaving town. I must have missed him along the way somewhere. Anyway, they have us now."

By this time Phil had the laptop up and was zeroing in on their location. "We're ten miles from the next stop area. There are two roads that cut off of this one before we get there. The one coming up in about three miles will give us the cut back capabilities. There are a number of secondary roads off of it and they head deep into the desert."

Jewell's attention was nailed down on the Corvette behind him. He could see it was a 2004 Vette and that would mean it was probably an above average road car. He was calculating the ability of the Mustang and its driving characteristic as compared to the Vette. The Vette was running an engine rated at between three hundred eighty-five to four hundred five horsepower with a top-rated speed around two hundred mph. The Mustang was rated around one hundred fifty-five mph. The question was could it, the Vette, handle off road?

Jewell was betting the Mustang was a better handling car. "All right, we'll take that road. The Vette could be faster than us, but I think we're better on the rough roads than it is. If I have this figured right, he has direct wireless contact with the other car or cars and so we will need to take him out. That means getting him in a situation where we have the advantage, we don't have it now.

"Now will that laptop tell you what the terrain out in that area is like and where the curves and wide spots are?"

Phil was working the key board like a mad man. He knew he had to get this right and do it in record time.

"Yeah, I've got it. When you get down that road two miles, take a hard right and then go less than a quarter mile and then take a hard left. The road will probably be hard pack when you get on it."

The Mustang started to accelerate and the Vette stayed right on top of him which is what he had expected. As they approached the turnoff, he could see that it was made for him.

He knew the Vette had the advantage being behind him, but that still gave him some advantages as well. One of those was that he knew where he was going and the Vette driver didn't.

He hit the corner at just around ninety miles an hour, sliding all the way. That was good enough, it caused the Vette to over drive the turnoff and that gave Jewell the time and space he needed to set this thing up. His mind was running off miles ahead of them and it included the next part of this game when they met up with the other carload of trouble.

The Vette driver recovered well and was back after him in seconds, but Jewell had the lead he wanted and needed. The next turn came up fast and right behind it was the left. He hit both perfect and asked the Mustang for everything it had.

The Vette was closing fast until they hit the second road. It was obvious that this was not a road-built car it was more of a touring model and didn't have the suspension he needed for these kinds of road conditions. On the other hand, the Mustang was in its element. It was eating the ground up like there was no tomorrow.

Jewell yelled at Phil, "Phil, get me a wide spot in the road around a curve or over a hill and do it fast." "Already have it, Jewell. You have two miles and you will go over a rise that drops twice as far as the climb on this side. It's perfect for our needs." Phil advised.

The hill came into view and Jewell gave the Mustang everything it could take. The road was rough and he needed to get over that hill, down the other side, and pulled over and out of the car before the Vette cleared the hill. It was all timing and it had to be right on the money.

They hit the hill and cleared ground going over it. When he landed, he braked and slid over to the side of the road. Phil was already bailing when the car stopped and Jewell was right behind him. Jewell ran across the road and Phil went to the back of the Mustang. They just got into position when the Vette cleared the hill and Jewell opened up on him. Phil followed suit and they literally cut the windshield out of its frame.

The Vette shot past them and then seemed to wobble and then shot out into the sage brush and swung sideways and then started rolling. It was over in just seconds. Jewell ran out to the car and Phil heard a single shot and then Jewell ran back and they got in the Mustang, turned around and headed back for the main highway.

"What's our next move," Phil asked.

Jewell could hardly talk because of the run and the amount of adrenaline running through his system at this time. "I want to go on around the stop area and then cut back to the stop and hit them from the east. They'll never see it coming."

They back tracked and then took the secondary east and around the stop where Jewell was sure the other car and people were waiting for them.

Phil asked, "How will we know which car is the one we're after?"

Phil sat there waiting for an answer when Jewell finally said, "They will be parked on the north side of the road facing east bound. There will be two men in it and the engine will be running. Their watching behind them for us to come around the bend and then the passenger will shove an automatic shotgun out the window and open up on us.

"That's their plan, but we'll be coming in from the east and they won't expect that. Phil, you're going to have to be fast on this one. When I yell now, you stick both guns out the window and cut loose on them.

"Empty your guns on them and then reload. Keep the rounds going in the passenger's window and don't stop till I tell you, got that?"

Phil was putting the laptop on the floor and getting his guns out and checking them. He dropped both clips out of the weapons and then loaded new fresh ones. By this time, they were turning back onto 80 west bound, he was ready.

The dark blue Mustang came screaming into the gas station stop from out of nowhere. The two guys in the green Chrysler didn't expect them to come in from that direction and by the time they started to react the Mustang was coming to a dead stop right alongside them.

Phil saw the barrel of the shotgun coming up when he opened up on the passenger. He saw the round pass in front of the passenger and hit the driver square in the side of the head, forehead high. The third and fourth round hit the passenger in the mouth and just below the ear. Both were dead in seconds. Jewell hit the gas, spun the Mustang around and floored it heading east bound.

The proprietor of the restaurant and service station had seen the green Chrysler sitting across the road and thought nothing of it. It was not until ten minutes later he heard the noise of a fast-moving car, brakes and then a series of gun shots and then heard a car pulling away at high speed.

By the time he got to the front of the station there was nothing out there except the Chrysler and a lot of smoke. He walked across the road and when he got to within five feet of the car, he could see the two men inside and he knew they were both dead. He ran back and made the 911 call.

With Phil's laptop tracking their progress and spotting any information that may hamper their progress, things went like clockwork. They would spend the night in Provo and head to Denver the next day. But they had to get to Provo first and the run-on Interstate 80 was now over and they would have to make other plans

Jewell continued east while Phil worked to pulled up a new plan and he found it. "When we get to Battle Mountain, you need to take SR-305 south. We will run it down to Austin, Nevada and then jump on to SR-50 and continue south." Jewell kept his speed nominal and when they reached Battle Mountain he turned south.

Phil kept the directions coming as Jewell continued south. "At the Junction of SR-50 and SR-376 turn east on SR-50 and then south on SR-50 at the SR-278 junction."

They came to Eureka and continued through on SR-50, then through the SR-379 junction and on through Ely, still going south.

"At the junction of SR-50 and SR-93

head south on SR-93, we need to tie back into Interstate 15 and then turn back north to Provo."

They passed through Pioche and then Panaca and on down and through Modena, then Beryl Junction and Newcastle. When they got to Cedar City, they got on to Interstate 15 and headed on up, northeast, to Provo.

They would spend the night in Provo and then planned on heading north into Salt Lake City, jumping on to Interstate 80 heading for Denver. That would put them back on track and back onto their plan. The only problem was they had left three more bodies behind them, and in short order that action would be on the news and their friends in Chicago would know the area they were in.

Once in Denver they planned on staying put for a couple of days. They would be heading south again for New Mexico and onto Interstate 40. The hope was their actions were as unpredictable as possible and would give them the ability to approach the Chicago area with the least number of problems.

But first they had to get to Denver and so they ran the Interstate 80 across the high plains through Wyoming. This gave them little traffic and set them up for entry into Denver from the north.

After reaching Denver they were ready to relax for a few days. They immediately started to watch the news for any shootings in the Nevada area. In a couple of days, they would start out on their next leg and head south on Interstate 25 to Albuquerque as planned and then turning east on Interstate 40 for Amarillo, Texas.

The plan was to remain in the Amarillo area for at least three days and prepare themselves for their next series of runs. Amarillo is located almost dead center in the Texas Panhandle. It is an old cattle town and has a population of around one hundred ninety-two thousand.

After finding a motel the two went to dinner and then back to their room to try and relax for a few minutes. This area was truly cattle country and the landscape supported it. You could stand on a spot and look for as far as you could see and not see a single tree of any size. It was said that a few years back the only really large tree on the panhandle, the hanging tree, had fallen over and died. Unless you were raised in this area, it was a place to visit and not stay.

In every battle throughout history there is almost always an unexpected event when isolated, means little. But, when looked at in relationship to the rest of the battle, it can change the whole outcome. That was about to happen here, in this old cattle town in the middle of the Panhandle. It seems that every time you let your guard down, that's when it happens and this time it happened in spades.

They didn't notice the SUV when it entered the restaurant parking lot. They, the occupants of the SUV, came in looking for a place to eat and they found more than they expected.

Jewell and Phil, we're getting in their car when the passenger of the SUV pointed at them. Jewell saw the gesture and recognized the driver. "Phil, in the car now, they've found us."

Both men were in the car and Jewell had it started and moving before the SUV driver could bring his car to a stop. Jewell droves straight ahead through an empty parking space and directly out onto 40 and headed west.

The SUV hit the road about three hundred feet behind them. Jewell had to keep his speed reasonable, but could see the SUV driver was pouring the gas on to try and get up to them. Just then they cleared the last traffic light going out of the city and Jewell floored it. The Saleen almost left the road it accelerated so hard. They left the SUV far behind them, but knew the game wasn't over yet.

Jewell called out. "Phil."

Phil was ready and looking behind them, "Yeah Jewell."

Jewell glanced over at Phil. "We can't just leave this behind us. We have to take these guys out and do it now. We can't leave anyone alive. If we do, they will let Benito know and he will know what we're up to, understand?"

Phil had already figured that out and was getting mentally ready for what he knew was coming, "Right."

Jewell started to lay the tactics out to Phil, getting him ready for the coming action. "All right, I only saw two in the rig so we should be able to handle them.

"If I slow down, they're going to know we're planning something. But we need to let them gain on us so that they will not lose us when we make the next turn. We need to maneuver them so that they end up in front of us so we can set them up.

So, we need to get behind them and take them out. Look their rig sits a lot higher than ours and that gives us an advantage. When we get behind them, I'll come up on the driver's side and you need to take out their left rear tire. Got me? Just roll the window down and point the gun and start pulling the trigger. That close and that many rounds will knock it out.

I'll then drop back and move to the right side and nail the other rear tire. That should disable them and then we have them." Phil was looking ahead and nodding his head, "Then what?"

Jewell continued laying out their actions. "Now listen to me. When we stop, get out of the car fast, as fast as you can and use the car door as a shield, when the passenger opens his door start shooting into it. He's going to keep coming out, so just pour it to him. Keep shooting until he goes down and then stays put. As soon as you've emptied your clip, dump it and put a fresh one in. Watch him, if he moves, hit him again. Got me?"

Phil's head was swimming with both anticipation and fear all mixed together. "I'll try Jewell, I'll try."

Jewell shook his head and yelled back at Phil. "Don't try, do it. Now, where's the next county road off this one?"

Phil checked and noted one to the left going south just a mile down the road. Jewell had slowed down some so they could catch up, at least within range so that they could see them. When the road came up, he took it and headed south. They saw the SUV take the turn.

Jewell told Phil to start looking for a place for their next move. "All right I need a canyon or something like that where I can find some cover to pull over and let them pass."

Two miles later it came and he slid in to the shadows of the rocks and came to a stop.

A minute later the SUV came by them at full speed. He hit the Saleen's accelerator and was onto the SUV before they knew what was going on. Phil rolled the window down and leaned out and opened up on the left rear tire. It came apart at the seams. Jewell braked and swung to the right and hit the gas and charged up to the right rear tire and opened up on it. As the .40 caliber rounds hit that tire it exploded.

The two in the SUV found themselves in front of the Mustang and then heard the shots going off behind them. They were confused and scared. The passenger rolled his window down and tried to lean out the window and get a shot at the Mustang but the bouncing of the SUV being exaggerated by the flat tire was making his task almost impossible. Then the right rear tire was lost and the SUV started to labor, really bucking.

He yelled at the driver to get the SUV stopped and they would take these two out now and finish this thing. The driver acknowledged and braked hard and brought the SUV to a stop.

Phil piled out of the car and ducked down behind the door and then brought his gun arm to rest on the top of the door and dropped his sights in on the passenger door of the SUV. Jewell was in the same position on his side.

They came out of the SUV guns spitting rounds as fast as they could. Phil saw the flashes, but heard nothing. He just started pulling the trigger. All he could hear was his gun going off in rapid fire. He could see the rounds hitting the door and then the guy came out trying to swing his weapon back toward

Phil.

He didn't know when the first round hit the guy and he had no idea how many had hit him. All he knew was that as the man's feet hit the ground his shoulder hunched up and he started to bend forward.

Next thing Phil knew he was dry firing and the guy was regaining his feet. His mind screamed at him. *The other gun, get the other gun going.* He swung his second gun up and cut loose. At this time, he could hear rounds going over his head and hitting the ground to his right. He had no idea if he was hitting anything. His mind had stopped working about twenty rounds ago, so he just kept on shooting.

Finally, after several hours the guy hit the ground, and there was no movement. Phil then glanced over at Jewell and he was in the process of standing up. He was no longer shooting.

Jewell yelled over. "Phil, load a new clip, now."

Phil was almost in a frozen state when he heard Jewell yell, "Oh, yeah."

He grabbed a clip off the seat and dropped the empty one out and loaded the new up. Meanwhile Jewell moved forward and he heard a shot. Then he moved back around behind the SUV and walked up to the second guy and fired one round into his head. He walked back to the Saleen and got in.

Jewell looked over at Phil and knew that he was having a small case of post battle syndrome. "Phil let's go." Phil was still standing behind the door looking at the guy laying on the ground and watching that muddy red patch of moisture growing second by second. Jewell finally got his attention and he climbed into the seat and sat back.

Jewell swung the Saleen around and headed back the way they came. They drove directly back to the motel and went in, got their belongings and left.

Phil was still trying to come out of the fog that had filled his brain by that time, "Where we going?"

Jewell was still working his plan and told Phil. "Oklahoma City can't stay here now. Need to just move out and get away from here. Phil, you did a damn good job back there."

Phil sat there looking at his hands, they were shaking and he couldn't make them stop. "I've killed at least four people in the past fifteen hours Jewell; I think I'm going to be sick."

That's all Jewell needed right then. "Lay your seat back and just relax, you'll be all right."

Oklahoma City was two hundred forty miles due east from Amarillo and they needed to get there before the bodies were found. Because it was late afternoon when the gun fight took place, they had a lot of time to get out of the state and into the greater Oklahoma City area. By the time they left it was starting to get dark. Phil kept checking the news agencies in the Amarillo area for any reports. At that point they were making good time and their luck was holding.

They crossed the Oklahoma border with no reports coming out of Amarillo. At Elk City Oklahoma they stopped for gas and Jewell checked the car for any damage. He was amazed that there was none.

At first, he did not find where a round had hit the car, and then he found one hit in the lower right corner of Phil's door. After looking it over it was obvious that it had not caused any significant damage.

Phil stood there and looked at the car shaking his head. "Jewell, how can that be?" God knows how many rounds were fired at them and only that one hit and then it only did minor, less than minor damage.

Jewell shook his head and looked over at Phil, "Just the luck of the draw Phil. Next time they could shoot the hell out of her and we would be left with nothing."

Phil stood there by his door looking at the car. He looked over the top of the Mustang at Jewell. "Hey, that's sixteen for you and four for me." He was actually counting the one guy killed in the Vette as one for each of them. Jewell thought to himself for a second and then nodded his head. "That's cool Phil, real cool."

Jewell smiled and got in the car.

Phil was finally thinking again and asked. "Jewell how do you think they found us?"

Jewell thought for a moment. "They were as surprised as we were. No, that was pure accident. Yes, they were looking for us, but they were not expecting to see us. They were too careless and thought that they could take us. That was in our favor.

"They hadn't planned for any kind of a run in with us. They also didn't expect the fire power we threw at them. No, those two were amateurs and they were looking for a big pay off and it cost them. The next ones may not be that poorly prepared."

So, the battle lines had been drawn. Their enemies had shown up and had demonstrated that they were out to kill them and nothing else. This is what Jewell felt it would be, a take no prisoners face off. Like any new recruit Phil had seen his first taste of battle and had survived. He had been directly involved and had fared well.

He was experienced now and from here on out it would be much easier, not that the killing of someone got any easier it was just that he would be able to do his job. There's nothing like experience by battle.

They knew now there was no other way to stop this, but to get to Chicago and kill Benito before they got killed. It was all or nothing. As they traveled toward Oklahoma City, they became even more committed to beating this game, whatever way necessary.

As they were driving on toward Oklahoma City Phil got to thinking about the gun battles and had noted something Jewell did and had done in the other fight back on 101 and in the desert. "Jewell, can I ask you something?"

Jewell looked over at him. "Sure, what

do you want to ask?"

Phil sat there a few seconds trying to determine how to ask something he knew nothing about. Finally, he asked. "Why do you shoot them in the head?"

Jewell sat there and thought for a few seconds. "Well, its insurance."

Phil asked. "Insurance?"

"Yeah, by putting a round through their head, they're sure to never wake up." Jewell continued. "I learned that years ago when I had a job in the north side of Chicago. The guy I was hired to take down was hit three times in the middle of the chest and I relaxed. Next thing I know the guy has me by the throat and is choking the life out of me. I managed to get another round into him, right through the side of his head and that ended it. After that I always fire an insurance round into the head."

In just a few days they had been in two fire fights, one in the Nevada desert and the other just outside Amarillo. The Nevada incident could be connected to them by the mob back in Chicago, if they took a close look at it, but Jewell doubted that the Amarillo fight would land on their table. It looked more like a local issue and not something tied to them.

As they approached Oklahoma City Jewell decided not to drive on through the main part of the city. He took the John Kilpatrick Turnpike around the city to Interstate 35 and headed north.

Outside the City area they found a motel and stopped. They needed to stay put for a time to see what comes out of the Amarillo area and then contact David and fill him in on where they were, but giving him no details or information as to what had taken place.

They were still eight hundred miles from Chicago by the shortest route, but had decided to head for Kansas City and then head east on Interstate 70 to St. Louis. From there they would jump on to Interstate 55 and go on into the Chicago area. They planned on staying in the western side of Chicago, staying away from Tinley Park.

So, the next three days would be spent working up their plan for when they get to the Windy City and finding Benito.

That last run to Chicago would be the most dangerous because Jewell would be getting back in to his home area and the risk of being seen would increase proportionally the closer, they got.

Finally, they were coming in on the last chapter of this Odyssey. The next process would determine their commitment to the plan, there was no other way. It was all or nothing and both were aware of that and were willing to face it that way.

Phil had contacted David, me, and filled me in on their current location and where they were heading next. Jewell had done well playing the game of chess with those out to find them. Now they had to go for broke.

Phil couldn't help but consider how they had gotten this far. In some respects, it was a minor or for that matter a major miracle depending on your own view point.

Now he knew what it was like for those who were facing their first time in a major battle. It made no difference if you were part of a military assault or two guys fighting for their lives. The feelings were still there. Could he, do it? What if he made a mistake or worse yet couldn't pull the trigger? The fear of failing was greater than the fear of doing nothing and simply cowering out of the game.

Still, he had performed well in the prior two incidents and had made his first kills.

Those still bothered him, but nowhere near how he felt about the officer that had been murdered by those first two guys.

He had learned to watch Jewell and pay close attention to his actions and his demeanor as he prepares for battle. He was pure business and looked like he had no fear at all. Yet, somehow Phil knew that Jewell feared as much as he did or any other person in their or similar situations. The difference was Jewell knew how to control his fear and channel it to his aggression and take advantage of it.

It was time, the last jump was ahead of them and they would then start the hunt. They were making that final jump from the prey to the hunter, the predator seeking and finding their prey and then starting the stalk.

The stalk, that point in the game where the predator actually put its nose to the ground and started the track. Searching out the scent of the prey's blood as it reached its nostrils and the taste of the kill on its tongue, the predator was coming to life and it meant the death of the prey. It was time for Checkmate.

The battlefield was strewn with the dead and there was more to come. It makes one wonder just how much any one man can take. Death had a way of taking parts of you even when you survive. After each battle you know a part of you did not come back, and you wonder how much more you can lose before you come completely apart. Few people realize that with each kill there is a price that is paid by the killer and it makes no difference if the kill was justified or not. Yes, Jewell knew how to deal with the art of the kill and that which followed but he still suffered that loss. Phil, he was feeling the loss and had yet to learn how to deal with it.

Checkmate, would it ever come or would it be by the opposition and not us. From now on there would be little sleep without the presence of the fear that takes up residency in you as you fight for your life.

Chapter Eight

THE HOME COMING

The news out of Amarillo reported two men being found on a county road ten miles west of the city. The television crew was at the scene where the police had recovered nearly sixty-four empty cartridges and the SUV with its rear tires shot out.

No names were given, so Jewell felt good that any relationship to them had not been established for the Benito family in Chicago. He knew that in time the report of the victim's names would be released, but that would not mean the mob would know they had been in that area and were probably heading toward Chicago. There was nothing in or around Amarillo that would tie Jewell and Phil to that area.

They left Oklahoma City early that morning, going north on Interstate 35 heading for Kansas City. It was between three hundred and three hundred fifty miles to Kansas City and they felt they needed to stay alert and make sure they avoided any location that would be attractive to Benito's soldiers.

Phil had been thinking about how they would be able to spot these people and asked Jewell, "Jewell how do you know where those people are more likely to be?"

Jewell was pleased with the growth of his partner and set out to explain how things worked in the world of the mob. "Phil those guys are on a mission and they take advantage of that. So, they eat at the best places, well what they consider the best places, and steak anywhere is the best. They stay in the best motels and drive the best cars they can find. While, we work hard at eating at the mom-and-pop restaurants and staying at the Motel Eights and Motel Sixes.

"Next, as of now we don't shave. Once the beards get a good start, we can trim them, but that is it. This will alter our appearance enough to make identification that much more difficult. It will give us an advantage. Are your guns loaded?"

Phil reached down and checked the location of his guns. "Yeah, and the clips are reloaded as well."

Jewell again was impressed with Phil's growth and preparedness. "Good. The only issue I had with you at the fight was that you failed to remember to load a new clip whenever the opportunity came.

"Don't worry about emptying each clip. After you've shot more than half of your rounds look for the lull where you can drop and load a fresh clip."

Phil was nodding his head and taking in everything Jewell said. "Got yah."

It was most interesting that in just over a three-week period two complete strangers had come together, under difficult and questionable circumstances, hit it off and managed to share their life stories with one another.

They began to meld into a partnership and a team. One was a committed killer, and the other a computer geek who didn't know one end of a gun from the other.

The master had taught the apprentice what he knew and would need to have in order to survive. The geek had managed to get through the last two battles as he watched the master ply his trade.

In the second battle the apprentice came into his own, now the master was tuning him to the point of being a well-trained, seasoned fighter.

It wasn't that Phil was not capable of doing these things it's just that he lived a sheltered life and all this was foreign to him. But, when the need presented itself and reality set in, he was as capable as anyone else of making that move to a true fighter.

It's odd how the survival instinct in all of us works. And, it didn't hurt that he was a natural with a hand gun. That was the one thing Jewell saw in him, a gun fit his hand as if he was born with one in his hand. He didn't need to aim. He put the sights on his target automatically and with deadly accuracy.

Phil was no longer that sheltered child. He had, in just over three weeks, seen eight people killed violently and without remorse. The death of the officer still haunted him and if for no other reason he was determined to deal with these people no matter what the circumstance or where it happens. To kill that officer just for the sake of eliminating a witness was the most outrageous thing he had ever seen.

Jewell's situation was not good. Whether defending himself or not, he had killed the son of the animal that was after them and that, in the end, had been the basic cause of the officer's death. Jewell accepted his part in the man's death and he too had a sense of revenge coursing through his body and he was going to make good for it if for no other reason than the officer.

Phil did not blame Jewell he just recognized that it was the gun battle that was the underlying cause and effect of this whole situation. In the end the two gunmen who had brought the officer into the situation were the ones responsible and they had paid the ultimate price for their actions.

Yet, he saw Jewell as a man of integrity. He was cold as hell, but up to this point he had been straight forward with him and that meant a lot. In the end Jewell would sacrifice everything to ensure Phil was safe even unto not saving his own hide. For the time being they were tied together and there was nothing either one could do about it.

In just over three weeks Phillip Morles has gone from a day-to-day geek, to a full-blown battle-hardened killer in his own right. Could he ever return to his prior life? That was a question he would need to address when and if he got out of this mess. For that reason, if none other, he had to do everything he could to kill Benito Cipozzio or die trying. Yes, he was tied to Jewell, but if he had been picking his own partner in this game, he couldn't have picked one better.

As they came into Kansas City, they used the same methods they had been using. They skirted the city and tied into Interstate 70 and then found a motel for the night.

They found a Motel Eight with a Denny's Restaurant next door and got a room. They walked over to the restaurant, ate and then returned to their room for the night. The day and evening had been uneventful.

The next morning, they would be on the road again heading for St. Louis some two hundred thirty-five miles east. Jewell was becoming more edgy as they drove closer to Chicago. There were so many people in the area that knew him or could identify him and the longer he was in that area the greater the probability that someone would mark him.

Again, Kansas City had been uneventful for them. They had driven around

217

the main core area of the city and had jumped on to Interstate 70 and pointed the car east and headed for St. Louis. All their planning and preparation had gone well and they were heading into the final leg of their journey to bring this game to an end, one way or the other.

Phil had seen the change in Jewell as they moved further northward and prepared to enter the greater Chicago area, "Jewell, you, all right? You seem a little edgy this morning."

Any one preparing to enter into a battle of any kind, anywhere, will show signs of nervousness. In this case Jewell was and knew it. "Yeah, I know. I can feel them. I can tell that they're out there watching for me and hungering for the chance to make a fortune"

Maybe it was Phil's inexperience or his failure to fully grasp and understand what they were getting in to. Because of that he failed to respond in a similar way, so he simply asked, "Who? Who are you talking about?"

Jewell's mind was reaching out trying to remember and bring each and every danger into focus. This was a whole new arena for Phil and he would need to know and understand their enemy. If there was any hope Phil had to adjust. Jewell replied. "Benito's boys, they're here somewhere, I just don't see them. I know a predator when I see and feel one because I am one and like will always recognize like."

Finally, that touched Phil and he began to recognize the magnitude of the task before them. "God, Jewell, you're getting me worried."

Jewell twisted in his seat and looked behind him. "You better be, we're in it now and it's going to get worse the closer we get to Chicago."

Phil moved back into his planning mode and asked. "Have you picked a location where we're going to hole up?"

Jewell had been thinking about that for some time and had worked everything out. "Yeah, I'm heading for Bolingbrook.

That's twenty-five miles from Chicago and is on the west side of the greater Chicago area. That's also about twenty-five miles west from Tinley Park and should be a good enough buffer area. It also gives us about an equal run time between both the big city and Tinley. That will work in our favor overall."

By mid-afternoon they were

219

approaching St. Louis and again skirting the town and moving north and tying into Interstate 55 to prepare for their final run to Chicago.

Jewell was still edgy and decided that he did not want to eat that evening. He felt it best that they stay away from any public place and in fact took great care in picking their motel for the night.

They found a motel with a ma and pa grocery next door. Phil went over to pick up a number of items that they could eat on during the evening.

Meanwhile Jewell was making sure he parked the car in a position that gave him the optimum access to the freeway and made it difficult for anyone cruising by to see it. He took everything out of the trunk and then marked the car before going into the motel.

It's an old trick he learned years ago. Set the car up so that if anyone tries to gain entry or messes around with it, they will disturb the marker and he would know someone had been there. Phil had been watching him and when he came through the door. "What was that all about?"

Jewell paused and looked back out the window. "I just want to make sure no one messed around with our car during the night. Just a little precaution now will ensure our success tomorrow."

Jewell finally turned to Phil. "Phil, let's talk. As we move closer to Chicago, we are going to be more vulnerable to discovery than any time in the past three weeks. Those other times were more based on chance than actual skill of the people looking for us, except for the Nevada thing. They had that scoped and set up well. We just lucked out because the Vette driver was stupid. But here they are looking for us and if they find us it will not be by chance.

"If they know we're here they will make every attempt to hunt us down and finish the game. Almost anyone I have known or who knows me could give us away it's all about money at this point.

"Benito knows a lot of people and believe me when I tell you that most, if not all, know that he is after me. If we're lucky they'll assume that we're in the southwest running for our lives and that gives us the edge. But that does not mean we shouldn't be on the watch for anything unusual.

"Simple survival tells us to keep a close watch on everything, if something looks out of place or just wrong, I need to know. Remember that. It may seem trivial to you, but it may be just the bit of information we need to keep us alive.

"Phil, you're into this thing up to your ever-loving chin and there is nothing you or I can do about it. So, watch and keep me informed. It's that simple."

Phil sat there mulling over what Jewell had just said. He was now realizing that everything they had gone through so far had been just the prelude to what was to come when they pulled into Chicago. This thing was nowhere near to being over and chance could be just as important as actual knowledge. Anything and everything were fully capable of killing them outright, so he had to get his act together and pay attention.

The next morning all was fine around the car. They loaded up and headed north on 55 for Bolingbrook. Jewell knew Bolingbrook well and had a number of close friends in that area. He had been thinking about contacting one or two, but decided to hold off on that until he had a chance to see how things were going there. Even though they were his friends that did not mean they wouldn't trade him in for the money Benito was offering for finding Jewell. No, the friends had to be left out of this thing. Temptation cannot be overlooked.

It had been almost two months from the day of the shoot out and he wanted to see if there were any issues openly taking place.

He also wanted to make a run by his house, at night, on the first days in the area. He would be looking for stake outs and questionable activity around the area.

If he found it then he could use that as a means of locating and then getting at Benito. At that time the stalk would start and it would not end until Benito was dead. There could be no other outcome. Even if it killed Jewell, Benito had to go and go now.

It was late afternoon when the dark blue Ford Mustang Saleen S281 Extreme pulled into Bolingbrook. This time they were going to find the finest motel in the area and set themselves up right, but that changed almost as fast as he thought about it, an apartment rental was the way to go.

They were now in the range of the man they were after. The contest was about to start and the instincts of the predator would soon make itself known. The game was about to start and the target of these predators would soon learn of his situation and face the reality that the end is coming down on him. If they were lucky that would come true at that moment when they hit Benito and he would die wondering what had happened.

Jewell knew of a location of upper-level furnished apartment rentals and he pulled into a station and called. They had two apartments left, one being a two bedroom and he took it. They drove over to the location and made the final arrangements and went up to their apartment and made themselves at home.

This would cover their presence in that area until such time that they wanted it to be known. He paid three months in advance at a cost of five thousand five hundred a month or sixteen thousand five hundred.

It was a perfect location and cover. For the first time in two weeks, they were able to relax and just let themselves get caught up with life. That evening, after dinner, they went to bed early. There was nothing planned for the next day so they planned on sleeping in and taking it easy for the day.

Late that night, after midnight, Jewell got up and left the apartment. He took the Mustang and headed toward Tinley Park. As he drove the distance between the apartment and his home, he had the opportunity to think over the coming days in the hunt for Benito.

It was quiet that night, there was little traffic and he saw no police units of any kind while driving to his home. He knew there was something wrong when he turned the corner onto his block. The location for his home was on a quiet neighborhood block with lower upper end homes all running in the five hundred thousand range on up. It was a perfect location for him and he loved it.

He planned on taking the next road left and going out and then coming back in on the other side as a means of checking for any cars or people staking his place out.

As he came around from the other direction, he didn't see his house, well he saw the lot, but the house was not there. As it really sunk in, he understood what had happened, they burned his house down. The lot had been cleaned up and only the foundation of the house remained. There was nothing else.

He pulled over to the curb and sat there looking at the empty lot. Everything was gone down to the last nail. He was not angry or hurt, that was the nature of the man he was facing. It made no difference whether Ben had been right, wrong or whatever, he was dead and Benito knew that Jewell had killed him. That was enough and that justified the burning.

After sitting there ten to fifteen minutes he resolved to move ahead and finish what needed to be done. Benito had to go, there was no other way. He thought back to his days as a youth and the many things that he and Ben had done, some perfectly all right and others highly questionable.

Yes, they were a couple of real winners back then. Ben could do just about anything and knew that his dads name covered and protected him. No one but no one would harm him under penalty of death, swift and direct. Benito made it clear, you attack or harm my son, and you attack and harm me. The really hard part about it was that Ben knew it and took advantage of it.

Jewell was no better because he stuck with Ben and took advantage of him and his protection. If Jewell was with Ben, no one touched him as well.

How did this all happen anyway? Jewell found it hard to remember just what pushed the button that brought all this to an end. He had been working with Ben on a big deal and if it had paid off, He, Jewell, would have been set for life.

No, it was that dumb little shop keeper and his refusal to pay what Ben wanted that started it all. God, he wished that he had done that favor for Ben and beat the little idiot half to death.

The whole of his life had been running with people like Ben and their spoiled lifestyles, taking advantage of anything and everything. He was a loner and would prefer being that way and now he was facing all that this life had brought on him.

Over these past weeks he had learned the real meaning of a friend and what life was all about and he did not like what he knew of his past. The truth was that it was easier to live that life style than to face what it actually meant and now that he was on the receiving end of the game, he had a whole new outlook on what his life had been.

No, he was going to end it once and for all and then leave every vestige of it behind him and start over. If he survived these next few weeks and got Phil home safe, then he would move to that spot by the Pacific Ocean and sit and listen to the waves tell him about the history of the world and the wonders that brought it to be. He would be that which he never was, but still hoped he would achieve, at peace with life and this world.

Phil felt like he could stay there in bed the rest of his life. It felt so good and he wanted to let time roll by and leave him to his dreams. He finally got up and took a long hot shower, dressed and went out to the living room. Jewell was there reading a paper.

Jewell looked up and then set the paper aside. "Good, you're up."

Phil was a little uncomfortable. "Sorry, did you want me up earlier?"

Jewell put Phil at ease and then got started. "No, it's just that we can get started. I took a quick run over to Tinley Park early this morning. They burned my house."

It looked like the restful day had been cancelled. Phil had heard him, but it didn't sink in right away, "They what?"

Jewell repeated what he had said. "They burned it to the ground."

Phil had a flash of anger and disbelief rush over him, "No way."

Jewell just sat there and stared off into nowhere. "Yeah, all the way down to the foundation. For that he is going to pay before I kill him."

Phil recognized the anger in Jewell and knew he could not let that happen. "Jewell, don't lose control now."

Jewell sat there still staring off into nowhere and then came back and looked at Phil. "I'm not, but I'm going to let him know when the right time comes, that I'm here and I'm after him. Now I want him to suffer. Now I plan on collecting my pound of flesh."

The look on Jewell's face was one of determination, but it was more than that. It was cold and emotionless. It was the look of a professional killer, one who was use to killing others.

It was a look that sent a chill through Phil's spine, Jewell then turned into the calculating and analyzing being that Phil had grown accustomed to. This man whose occupation was one for the books and a life that was equally mind bending. The thought passed through Phil's mind that he sure as hell didn't want to be on the receiving end of Jewell when he was mad. For a second there he felt sorry for old Benito

Phil saw the change and shifted into the planning mode himself. Yes, the restful day would not be. "Jewell, what are you planning?"

He looked at Phil, this time with the coldest and deadliest look Phil had ever seen in any human being. "First of all, I want to know are you with me all the way?"

Jewell's eyes were stone hard and Phil knew that the moment of truth was at hand. He either took the jump or he ran. They stood there looking at each other for several seconds then Phil offered his hand to Jewell. Jewell reached out and took it and they stood there tightly gripping each other. No words were necessary.

In a soft, controlled voice Jewell started the planning phase of their return. "Starting tomorrow we will be gathering information on the Cipozzio family.

I want you to get on your computer and start finding everything you can on him, Benito. Everything Phil, is there anything you're going to need to get that job done?"

Phil mind started running at full speed as he thought of what he needed to set him up and get started. "Yeah, I need a printer. A good one that is capable of photo printing and two-sided printing."

Jewell jotted that down on a tablet he had picked up that morning. "All right, we'll go shopping for a printer first thing."

Jewell then added to the list. "While we're at it we'll pick up a good camera with telephoto lenses and a good set of binoculars. While you're doing the computer research, I'm going out to get some surveillance work done.

I need to find Benito, his home, those who are with him and get shots of every one of them. If everything goes right, they will be where they have always been.

Phil was getting more concerned about Jewell's venturing out of the apartment heading into enemy lines. "Jewell, be careful and when you do see him control yourself."

Jewell looked at Phil. "Look, I've done this before. Believe me, when I take him, it will not be a spur of the moment reaction. No, don't worry about that. It will happen when it's supposed to happen. Phil, I appreciate your concern for me, but this is my business. We're in my realm now and I can function in it as well as you can breathe. No, I'll be careful and I'll treat this job just as I always do as a professional."

So, they had it set. Phil would do the internet research on Benito and Jewell would do the on-the-scene surveillance of the bunch.

They had given themselves a week to bring all the data together and then start laying out a plan. The object was to take out Benito, and if anyone else got in the way then they would go as well.

In addition, Jewell wanted Benito's home destroyed before they hit him. That would be the final touch, the destruction of Ben's home as well. Phil felt that they were taking on a lot and they may be better off concentrating on Benito. Jewel was adamant, he wanted it all, but he realized that greed now could kill them.

So, there it was. Jewell had made it home without any fanfare or being found out. On the way eight people had died, one being a police officer who had been used by the mob to stop Phil's car and then shot down to eliminate him as a witness.

Jewell was on familiar ground now and he was at home moving around the area and dealing with those who would be a danger to him.

In the past he was just another one of the inhabitants, but now he was a predator. He had his prey determined and the hunt was on.

Now he was in his realm, the jungle that he was so accustomed to, the jungle outside the law and the lives of the average resident living in the greater Chicago area.

His prey had a name, Benito Cipozzio. It had a tribe the Cipozzio Family, and it had a clan the Mob, Mafia, La Casa Nostra. And as with any predator, it was a hunt to the death of either one or both.

And, as with any predator he would depend on stealth and the fact that his prey was not aware of his presence.

There is little defense against something like that, an attack out of nowhere with no warning and no understanding as to what was going on, an attack that would be fast, brutal, and targeting one and only one end, the prey's death. That is all the predator is after, no more and no less. That is its life, its purpose, its destiny.

Unlike a pride of predators hitting a herd, this was a one-on-one tracking and stalking of the prey. A deliberate, calculated, and emotionless act of savagery, targeting one and only one being, and that was a being that was as deadly and dangerous as the predator was. It would be lightning fast, direct targeting, and with a level of finality that even the prey would recognize and understand.

In the end everyone knew that it had to come down to this. Benito was giving no leniency to the issue. He was dead set on achieving the death of Jewell and anyone and everyone that had anything to do with him after the death of his son Benjamin.

It was more than just his son it was the name. No one dishonored the name of Cipozzio. The honor of the family was at stake and no matter how many must die it will be avenged. Even at the cost of the old man himself.

Chapter Nine

PREDATORS AND PREY

When carrying out intelligence gathering there is no way of knowing what that intelligence you receive or discover will provide. The majority of it is just background information. Nice to have, but of little real planning value.

On the other hand, the most innocuous bit of information may carry the total success of the plan. It works that way. So, any good scout will collect it all and then work out each piece's value later on.

So, it was with Phil and Jewell. They collected everything and anything that pertained to Benito and his family.

Newspaper articles, legal documents that were available. Census data, banking data, real estate data, all of it was collected and gathered together in one place.

The make and model and license numbers of every car he owns or did within the last five years. This included his physical condition and problems including his age and marital status and any and all children alive and living with him or nearby.

It all goes into the basket and then they start the evaluation. They gave themselves a week to collect and prepare all the data on their target. Once that was done the job then was to sort and organize the data and then start the analysis for the operation.

Any predator knows that the more it knows of its prey, the greater the odds of success when tracking it. To know your prey is the most important part of the hunt.

That knowledge tells you what his habits are, what his dislikes are, who he keeps around him, and what his demeanor is. That is attitude and temper. Each and every bit of information goes into the making of a complete picture of the prey and also tells the predator when and where to attack.

The name of the game is total control,

leaving no edge or means of escape available to the prey. Creating a plan which places the prey into a situation where whatever moves it makes it moves deeper into the trap and finds no way out.

The idea being that the prey has no chance of survival, no matter what it tries or does. It's the development of a kill zone that is inescapable, that once in it the prey is aware that there is no way out and that it's time to die has come.

Jewell wanted that moment more than anything else in his life. He wanted Benito to know this was it and he was going to die.

The process of moving around in the world of Benito's can be dangerous, especially if you're not paying attention and using common sense. Jewell stalked each individual on a one-on-one basis, collecting his photos and any and all information that was out there. He moved during the day and even more during the night. Slowly closing in on each one and getting what was needed for what was to come.

He was careful not to be seen in the same place more than two or three times. He did not want to draw anyone's attention to him. It was important that he remain invisible, not there, he had to be that non-being, that creature living among his prey unseen and unknown.

On the morning of day eight Phil and Jewell sat down at the table with a pile of papers before them. Every piece of information on Benito and his Mafia Family that they could collect was laying there.

They had placed a bulletin board on the wall so that they could mount photos and vital documents for the planning. The next weeks would be spent studying and making additional forays to verify details and target activities.

The first to appear on the board was the photos of Benito, the Boss or Capofamiglia, followed by his Advisor or Consigliere, then the Under Boss or Sotto Capo.

Then the Captains or Caporegime and finally the Soldiers, below the soldiers were the wannabes, also known as Associates.

In addition, the Boss would have a bodyguard and a driver, sometimes one individual was both. In Benito's case he had a driver and a bodyguard.

He had a total of four Caporegime, or Captains, with eighteen to twenty soldiers under each one of them. That gave him seventy-two to eighty soldiers plus the four Caporegime.

All in all, he had an organization of two hundred ninety-two to three hundred twenty-four people under him, not counting any associates he may have hanging around under the soldiers. When you added his Sotto Capo, Consigliere, driver and bodyguard they had a total of two hundred ninety-six to three hundred twenty-eight made members in the Cipozzio Family.

Benito's main mode of transportation was a 2003 Lincoln Continental Limousine. This car he almost always drove in going to work or doing anything Family related. I guess you would call it his official signature of power. On occasion he and his driver would be seen in a 2003 Chrysler 300, going golfing or making a short run to his favorite restaurant, it was his unofficial personal mode of transportation. Records indicated that he had three other cars, but these appeared to be more collector cars than day to day users.

His home was located in an area just south of Chicago on a bluff overlooking Lake Michigan. The total area of the compound was ten acres, all of which was manicured and well maintained.

The house itself consisted of twenty-eight rooms with a ten-car garage attached. The entire compound was walled and fenced off with a fully automated gate at the driveway entrance. It was obvious that the compound was well protected with the use of video cameras.

At least eight cameras were visible from the street. The compound was a fort, not a home. To even get onto the compound grounds would be a major issue. No, this was a stronghold and one that could not be breached by just two people. The idea of destroying it also fell by the wayside. Any desire to do that would jeopardize the whole of the plan and so it was thrown out.

He, Benito, had four businesses in the lower south end. One was a real estate business, with offices located on a major arterial road in front of it. It was managed by a professional and appeared to be a legitimate operation. Legitimate? Yes, mob bosses do have legitimate business interests and those were activities that were never good for a hit. It was marked as a no-go spot.

The next two were night clubs in the lower end and on the main entertainment strip, one on S. Commerce Avenue and one on S. Torrence Avenue. Benito spent a lot of time at these two locations, but he had no dependable schedule for being at either place.

Besides that, these were places that were always full of family members and members of other families in the city. Any action that could harm or kill another family member or made man would simply end up having another group of hunters on their tail. No, these too were not conducive to what they were planning there were just too many people and too many unknowns to deal with.

The fourth place was a hole in the wall bar that was located on a side street in a rather run-down area. This place was his main office for the operation of his family business. The fact was that it matched the animal they were after. The den of the creature that had brought about this whole issue, and that place was crawling with his army.

Here he spent the better part of the day, but here too were the majority of his family organization, either on the premises all day or coming and going continually day and evening. There could be anywhere from five to twenty soldiers in or around that location at any given time. And that was six days of the week. But Sundays were free and open.

Finally, the first element of the plan came together, Sunday. Believe it or not, bosses like Bonito honor Sundays as special days. There was no business on Sunday and if there ever was it was of a nature that even the government didn't want to see happen. Sundays were a day of rest and Benito took total advantage of it.

The next issue was which Sunday would be the best one for the hit, but that would depend on what he did on Sundays and which activity took place on which Sunday.

As it turned out he almost always played golf on Sunday, in the morning. His tee time was set and reserved for him and his party each and every Sunday. He played Golf at the Ravisloe Country Club located in Homewood, just southwest of his home.

Each time he had the same foursome, including him, none of which were members of his mafia family. They were all business men from the locale area.

Further checking on the three business men determined that they were clearly not associated with Benito's criminal empire, but were tied through his real estate business. That limited their ability to target him on the course. They wanted to ensure that no

242

innocents were hurt, no collateral damage.

Jewell made a trip through the parking lot of the country club to get an idea as to the extent of the lot, the number of parking places and the access into and out of the lot. The place was restrictive in their ability to enter and exit it. Not a good spot for an assault. The country club sight was eliminated as an attack point.

However, they determined that after his golf outing, he and his driver always went by the local pizza restaurant and picked up a large deep-dish pizza to take home. As they watched, they determined that each Sunday they stopped at the same pizzeria and picked up the same pizza. The only issue there was that the pizzeria always had the pizza ready when they arrived and the driver was only in the store a few minutes while picking it up.

Jewell sat back. "Wouldn't you know it, the simplest and smallest of things determines the fate of someone. Who would have thought that a simple pizza would be the key to a killing? We've got him."

Now the planning really moved into high gear. They had been at it now for two weeks and it was time to set a date, time, and location. That would depend totally on what they had to do in preparation. They needed to make an in-depth study of the pizzeria, the street it was on and the surrounding businesses.

The location had been determined along with the day. Now they had to pick which Sunday to do it and determine the actual time of the selected day and that was going to have to be a time range and not a specific time. When Benito and his driver arrived at the pizza restaurant, they would be able to take him with little if any problem.

The driver will go into the place and pick up the pizza, about five minutes at the most and in all probability less. In that time, they will take Benito out. When the driver comes back to the car, they will finish him and then leave. The exit onto the street was wide open and going right was perfect for them. It was set, now they had to do the dry runs.

They went out to the Mustang and headed out for Homewood and the pizza place. At first, they simply drove by and checked the place out. They were looking for surveillance cameras in the parking lot. They saw none.

Next, they checked the businesses on

either side of the restaurant and then across the street. They identified three cameras on the block the pizza place was on.

Next, they needed to know the angle of the cameras in relationship to the road and the pizza place. They determined that two of the cameras were targeted directly into and toward the businesses they were mounted on. They had no view of the street out front.

The third camera was at the back of a used car lot pointed toward the street but angled down at the cars in the front row. That camera was on the opposite side of the street from the pizza place. Based on that they were fairly sure they were free of any video observation.

The one issue that was still to be worked out was whether they would be using the Mustang or finding another vehicle to use and then abandon it when they were finished. If they used another car then they would have to find an exchange location where they could leave the attack car and move back to the Mustang and leave the area.

The first question was how to get the other car. They could lease one, but that would leave a record of who leased the car. They could steal one and then make sure they left no evidence inside and then dump it at the exchange location. Then of course they could use the Mustang. If they were identified it would be strictly luck of the draw and they could live with that.

Finally, they settled on the stolen car scenario. With that they needed to find an exchange location, one that had little, if any traffic, and had ease of access for getting to the nearest freeway.

They decided to go out around the area where the pizza place was located and scout for a good exchange location. They finally found a park where there was plenty of room and substantial parking. The ideal thing about this park was that it had a lot of wooded areas the roads went through and in those wooded locations there were three to five parking spots. That was perfect. The park was in an upper social structure area with numerous high-priced homes.

They finished preparing the backup plan for the disposal of the stolen car, a disposal bag and a first aid kit in the event someone got hit.

The disposal bag was designed to be used when they abandoned the stolen car. Basically, it was a small ignition unit with a container of fuel. Once the vehicle was left parked that item would be placed in the car and activated. They would have five minutes to clear the area before it set the car on fire.

The first aid kit had several plastic sheets and other bandages and cleaning supplies. It was not meant to be a full-blown treatment or triage bag, just enough supplies to stop and control bleeding.

Back at the apartment they were now ready to lay out the final schedule and assignments for the hit. Jewell made it clear that he would do the job. Phil's job would be to drive the stolen car to the location and stand by while Jewell carried out the assault. If everything went right, they would be leaving the lot in less than sixty seconds and will have left two dead bodies in the parking lot, oh and one dumped deep-dish pizza.

Everything had been timed out. They planned on being at the pizza place at least thirty minutes before Benito and his driver were expected there.

They needed an hour to locate and take the car, go to the exchange locations, leave the Mustang and then go to the pizza place. So, that worked out to half an hour to Homewood from their apartment, an hour to find and take the attack vehicle and go to the Mustang drop off point. Then they needed a half hour to get to the pizzeria and setup for the hit. They planned on being at the pizzeria a half hour before the hit. That worked out to two and a half hours from when they left the apartment to the pizzeria.

Phil was double checking the distance and time elements as Jewell laid it out. Now they had to find the stolen car. Between Bolingbrook and Homewood, it was twenty-three miles. They would be able to locate and obtain a car anywhere along that route.

A predator always has its favorite area that it wants to hunt in, this area was Jewell's and he knew it well. Once the predator identifies the prey, it becomes its total focal point. Absolutely nothing else will interfere in its pursuit of the prey. All that it exists for is that prey and nothing else. All it wants is the taste of the prey's blood in its mouth and the smell in its nostrils. At this point its entire being changes to a savage, blood thirsty creature that will die in its quest to find, run down, and take its prey.

You can read it in its eyes and see it in the scruff of its hair around the neck standing and signaling its blood-lust.

It was a process of total commitment to the hunt. The prey will fall or the predator will fall trying. There is no latitude for failure. To fail is to die and there is nothing else on its mind. It's not an evil thing it's what is natural among all predators, the rules of life that one kills or is killed.

One dies for the continuation of life and one lives through that death and the bounty it results in, whether animal or human the mindset of the predator is the most basic savage existence. The prowl of the wolf begins.

The day of the wolf was set at two weeks from then. As a contingency plan, if it, the hit, fell through they would target the following Sunday.

Jewell spent much of his time prowling around the area between Bolingbrook and Homewood. He drove the area during the time of day the hit was set for, paying close attention to traffic flows and pedestrian activities.

On Sundays he did the same noting the differences between weekdays and Sundays. Every detail was checked and rechecked. He had one chance and he meant to make it count.

Phil zeroed in on tracking the weather and any special public events that might be taking place at that time. He was looking for special sales and promotional activities in the area of the hit and the route to that area. He was watching for information on police emphasis activities in the same areas. Last thing they wanted to do was run head long into a mess of cops working traffic, especially in a stolen car.

The plan was a good one and Phil and Jewell knew that if all went right, they would complete their task, the only question that remained was, would that end it. Surely, the family would leave it alone.

The Under Boss would become the new family head and surely, he would not care that much about the outcome of Benito's life. They were that way, always looking for that edge, the means of stepping up and taking over. It was one of those things, where they were loyal to the family, but their loyalty to the boss was always in question.

The real problem was Benito's two close soldiers, the driver and his bodyguard. They would fight back and they would be expert in the art of battle.

They would be the most dangerous of

all the soldiers in the family. It was important to know these two and the research had done just that. Know your enemy better than you know your friend. Your friend is not the threat, your enemy is.

The driver, Anthony Carbon, was a longtime associate of Benito. His father had been a close friend of Benito until his death in a mob war some years back. Benito had promised to take his son under his wings and that he did, making the young Carbon his driver.

With that came the training and teaching in all aspects of being a direct assistant to the boss. He was dedicated to his position and never disappointed the old man in any way. He would die before letting anyone harm Benito.

Carl Sarcina was probably one of the best and strongest bodyguards in all the Chicago area. He was known for his cold efficiency. He would kill you first and then ask questions.

If you touched the old man without being given permission, he would break your arm or leg. No warning, no second chance. It made no difference what the weapon was he was proficient and deadly in its use. It would take more than a good shot to stop him, it would take half a dozen good shots to put him down.

Normally the bodyguard stayed at the compound when the old man went to play golf. The driver naturally went, but remained with the car while the boss played golf.

Why they did this was not known. It could have been the impression it may have made on the other golfers.

It could be that the country club did not want armed personnel walking around the facilities. Whatever the reason, half of the old man's protection would be absent.

Still, that meant that Carl would be out there and he would come looking for whoever did the old man in. He would not stop and they would have to deal with him.

That would have to wait right now, it was Benito and nothing else. Yet, the predator knew the heart and mind of a predator and that meant Carl would be looking for them and it could only end one way.

When the job was done, they would have to start their planning for dealing with the bodyguard, who had an oath of death to pursue and get those responsible.

Time is a strange thing. When you want

it to move along slowly it charges like the end of all time was drawing near.

When you want it to speed up it just lays there looking at you. It drives you to distraction and then turns around and smacks you square in the mouth. The time between their preparation and the actual assault should have passed quickly, but it crept along, stopping at every flower and taking a long sniff.

Phil was clearly showing the effects of the wait. He was even losing weight and that was not good. He just couldn't help it. "If this thing doesn't end soon, I'm going to shoot myself." Phil said.

Jewell would keep his voice cool and calm when addressing Phil's nervousness. "Easy guy, it's just time. When it gets here, you'll be wishing that there was more time for you to ready yourself. Don't think about it. Just try to relax and take each and every moment and enjoy it. Remember, this job is not a sure thing. We could still get killed without even trying hard. Learn to appreciate every day, every hour, and every minute as it comes and goes."

What should one think about when their considering or are involved in the actual taking of the life of another person? This is not a firefight initiated by someone else. This is a planned, fully thought-out assault on an individual who they had marked for death.

It was a challenge to work the plan up, but it was becoming even more of a challenge to carry it out. Fortunately, Jewell would be doing the actual assault.

Phil sat there looking at Jewell. He was studying this man and trying to determine what made him tick. He was driven, yet there was this coolness about him. Fully prepared, but completely relaxed. If there was stress, he was good at covering it up.

Phil realized that personal control was the mark of the professional. He who could keep calm and controlled while preparing and waiting for the main event was usually the one that walked away from the encounter. Jewell had learned through hard knocks what it meant to be controlled and at ease with one's self as this time passed. It was almost as if he actually controlled time itself that each minute as it came and went had to get permission from him to do just that.

Finally, the day was approaching. It was a Friday afternoon and they went over their plan one last time. Jewell had decided that he wanted to take a scouting run Saturday afternoon into the area between Bolingbrook and Homewood to see if he could spot a likely car to take on Sunday morning. He knew what he wanted, but opportunity would be the rule in this case. If he found the specific car he wanted, then they were set. If not, he would have to look for a backup car.

Basically, they wanted a car that was not unusual, a car that is seen all the time by people walking and driving the street. He preferred a white or gray car, midsize four doors. Engine size was not an issue, but it had to be dependable.

He found his target car parked in a lot behind a church not too far from the freeway. It was the right make and color and had not been parked too long. That was marked as their number one selection.

He then looked for and found another similar vehicle a block further down the street in another parking lot. That would be their back up in the event the first one was not there. They were set.

The stress of the wait was growing moment by moment. They went over their places and times again, making sure that they left nothing out. Phil was having the hardest time keeping his head together.

He was becoming unsure of his ability to carry this out. Jewell found he was continually re-talking Phil back into the plan and easing his conscience about the whole thing. It was becoming a major concern for Jewell. He needed a second man. Anyone else from this area was out of the question. No, Phil had to be there.

Jewell had considered doing the job himself, but there were just too many unknowns that could screw things up and one person would not be able to deal with them. No, Phil had to come and he had to perform and perform well.

Jewell finally turned to Phil. "Hey, look at me. Are you listening to me? Phil, are you listening to me?"

"Yeah, I am."

"All right, now you have got to get yourself under control. We have come this far and we only have a short time to go. Phil, this has to be done. I'm telling you that if we don't do this, we're both dead men. I'll be able to last longer than you. They'll simply eat you for breakfast."

Finally, Jewell said. "Phil, unless we do this, I cannot protect you. It simply won't happen, if we run now, it's every man for himself."

Phil was nervously rubbing his hands together. "Yeah, but they don't know who I am."

Jewell shook his head and pointed at Phil. "Phil, they do."

Phil was finding it hard to believe that they knew who he was. How could they know that, he had never been around here before and none of the others knew who he was? "How?"

Jewell smiled at the naivety of Phil and simply said, "Your car."

Phil had not expected that and had half way forgot about his car. "What?"

Jewell tried to drive home the issues. "Phil, your car, we left it at the shooting where the officer was killed, remember. They know who you are and that you are with me. You're marked and there is nothing we can do about it until we deal with Benito. Do you understand?"

Phil sat there and looked off into space. Damn, he had forgotten about his car. How could he do that, it was so stupid? Man, he was really into this and there was no turning back

Jewell was trying to get Phil's attention and reached out and touched his arm. "Phil?"

Phil snapped out of his thoughts and looked at Jewell. "Yeah, Jewell, I heard you and yes, I understand. I just forgot about that. I was sitting here thinking, how could I forget that? Damn!"

Jewell knew what he was going through. He had been there at one time early on when he was first entering into his career choice. "All right now, get it together, you're driving the car and nothing else. That is unless I get hit and then you have to take care of both of us, Got me."

Phil's mind moved back into his place and responsibility to Jewell, "Right."

Jewell, the master leaned in close to Phil. "Phil, I'm depending on you, so get your head together and start thinking. Remember what I told you, if I get back to the car and get in on my own, then get us the hell out of there.

"If I go down, get out. Take off. Go back to the Mustang and burn the stolen car and head back to the apartment. Take the money out of my suit case, shave and grab your belonging and leave.

"Just get the hell out of Illinois before

the news of the hit is broadcast. That's all you have to do Phil, so get it together and let's get ready."

After that, the days seemed to move by fairly fast. The final prep work was completed. Jewell had made sure the Mustang was fully fueled and he knew where the number one and two target cars were located.

They then set to work preparing their weapons. Usually, it's not a big deal. You clean the gun and you load it and put it away. This time Jewell made sure every part was clean and working properly. There was no room for jams or failures, they had to work perfect. All ammo was wiped down as it was loaded into the clips and each clip was wiped down.

They finally got to bed after midnight. That was no problem because neither one could have gone to sleep prior to that anyway. Phil slept fitfully during the night. He finally fell asleep around three and then went in to a deep worn-out sleep.

Jewell on the other hand slept peacefully all night long and was up at six that morning. He decided to let Phil sleep as long as possible. They would be leaving the apartment around noon in order to be able to get the target car and then be stationed at the pizza place before Benito and his driver got there.

Meanwhile, he worked up the rest of the kits and maps and got ready to move everything out to the car. At nine he got Phil up and finished getting ready himself. While Phil was finishing up Jewell got a breakfast ready and then sat Phil down and made him eat. After eating and while sitting at the table Jewell looked at Phil. Jewell was deliberately slowing things down at that moment in order to give Phil the chance to collect himself, "How you doing?"

Phil found that he was refreshed and also, to his amazement, feeling good and ready to go. "Right now, I'm feeling fine."

Jewell brought him back to reality. "You ready for this?"

Phil sat there nodding his head and then he sat up straight and said, "Yeah, about as ready as I'll ever be."

Jewell smiled and reached out offering his hand to Phil and Phil reached out with his and they shook hands and wished each other luck. "All right, let's get going."

This was not unlike a military maneuver and it carried with it all the timing and planning that any maneuver would call for. What had been a nervous and hard to deal with process had now turned into a cold, calm and deadly process. The butterflies were still there, the time passed and now it was a matter of doing it.

There comes a time when all the planning and scouting in the world does nothing to advance a plan or project. Now it was time for carrying it out and there was no turning back. It was time and the pack was ready and eager to move on.

Had they forgotten anything? Well, if they had it was too late now. It was time. Any omissions they may have made would have to be made up for as they were discovered during the hit. If they had planned well, and Jewell was sure they had, they would have no surprises.

His only real unknown was Phil and that could not be changed. Phil had to take part and he had to do as directed. If he failed then they both failed and they would go down together and Benito would come out the victor. Jewell bit his lower lip and promised himself he would not let that happen, no matter what.

So, this was it and there was no turning

back. All the traveling all the fighting and all the hard times were now behind them. It was now or never.

Chapter Ten

DAY OF THE WOLF

They left the apartment parking lot at eleven, on the nose. Phil was driving and Jewell was giving him directions to the location of their primary target car. As they turned the corner the car was sitting there where it had been. There were other cars on the lot but no one was around. Being a Sunday Jewell had expected other cars in the parking lot. The plan was that they pick the car up while church was in session thereby avoiding anyone seeing them. Jewell exited the Mustang and walked across the lot to the car.

He popped the door and got in and

wired her up. As the power hit the dash, he could see that she was three quarters full of gas, perfect. He started the car and put it in drive and exited the lot with Phil close behind in the Mustang. Stage one was completed with no complications.

They drove on over to the Van Horne Woods Forest Preserve and found the parking spot for the Mustang and parked both rigs. They had seen no other vehicles as they came into the Preserve. Jewell transferred the burn bomb and aid kit from the Mustang to the target car and then got into the Mustang with Phil. Stage two now completed.

Jewell was all business and started to cover the action again with Phil. "All right, everything is going just fine, we're ahead of schedule. In twenty minutes, we'll leave here in the other car and head down to the pizza place. We've got the burn bomb and the aid kit, so I think we're covered."

The weather was actually perfect for this job. It was cool and cloudy which made it difficult for people to see much detail. In addition, people seldom wandered in these wooded parks unless the weather was good. It was a Sunday and people normally had other plans in the morning hours. Park activity wouldn't pick up until the afternoon.

When they had entered the park, they saw no other vehicles or people in or near the park. The further into the park they went the darker it got and the less chance of seeing anyone there. It was perfect.

Finally, it was time. They left the Mustang, locked it up and headed out. If all went well, they would be back in less than an hour. It took about twenty minutes to drive down to the pizza place. They pulled into the parking lot and set up for the job. Stage four successfully completed.

There were few cars in the lot, but at that time church had not let out, when it did people showed up for their afternoon meal. They were depending on having a lot of cars and people in the area when they hit Benito. Confusion always helps blinding witnesses.

Overall, the traffic coming to the pizza place had been light, again due to the time of day. It was turning out to be a perfect time and location for this kind of job. Jewell had been watching Phil and so far, Phil was rock hard and showing no signs of the nerves he had shown during the week prior. Jewell had a good feeling about how this was going to go down. He knew they had a better than even chance of getting away with little or no injuries.

By twelve thirty the lot was about a third full. If Benito kept to schedule, he would be pulling into the lot in about fifteen minutes. Jewell checked his weapons again and started building himself up for the job.

The weather was holding and people were not spending a lot of time in the lot. If coming in they went right into the place. If leaving they went directly to their cars and left. Everything was just right.

Ten minutes later a Chrysler 300 pulled into the lot slowly making its way from the street and round to the end of one of the parking lanes and stopping in the no parking area at the end of the lane. They had parked across from the main entrance to the restaurant so that the driver had less distance to walk and he remained within a reasonable distance from his boss.

The driver got out and headed for the front door. Jewell, at the same time, exited the stolen car and started walking toward the Chrysler. This was it; all the planning and preparations was now paying off. They had their prey grounded and all that needed to be done was the final assault and that was on the way.

Almost two months of running and hiding and planning was coming to an end. Jewell was twenty feet from the car and already pulling his guns out. Phil watched the front door and had exited the get-away car and preparing himself for any action. Just then Jewell got to the Chrysler, reached out and grabbed the door handle and jerked it open.

Nothing is more paralyzing than when someone is taken by surprise, totally unexpected and that was the situation Benito was in. He had no recourse, there was no place he could go he was incapable of fending for himself. The terror filled eyes of the prey was staring straight in to the piercing eyes of the predator.

Jewell leaned in bringing his face directly into Benito's face and driving the fear deep into him. At the same time, he is bringing his gun in his right hand up and shoving it directly into Benito's chest. Phil could see that Jewell was saying something to Benito. It was a face off that only time was delaying and one that would bring the lives of these two men into total focus and finality. Just then three flashes went off. Phil did not hear the shots he just saw the flashes and

Jewell's arm recoil from the rounds going off.

That was followed by a fourth flash and then the rear window of the Chrysler turned red, the head shot had been made. Jewell was still leaning into the car and Phil was beginning to wonder why the delay in his exiting and getting back to their car.

Phil's attention was drawn to the front door of the pizza joint as the driver came out the front door. He had the pizza in his left hand and was concentrating on closing the door behind him when he turned and immediately saw a man leaning in the front door of the car. You had to give him credit he saw the scene in front of him and immediately reacted. He dumped the pizza and shoved his right hand into his jacket and started to draw his gun and bring it up.

Across the lot Phil had seen the driver exiting the pizzeria and he hit the horn of the stolen car and started to swing around and target in on the driver. Jewell heard the horn and instinctively knew that trouble was behind him and came up and out of the car bringing his weapon up onto the driver.

The situation was all laid out with Phil to the drivers left, zeroing in on him and Jewell dead ahead of the driver and bringing his weapon up out of the car and dropping it in on the driver. The driver had already cleared his holster and had his weapon leveled on Jewell.

All three hammers dropped at almost the same time with Phil's being just a flash of a second ahead of Jewell's and the driver. It was a triangle of death and the driver was out gunned and he knew it so he concentrated on the man at his boss's door.

The first round from Phil's gun came in on the driver and hit him in the left leg his second round came in high and hit the driver left shoulder. Phil was the first of the three to open up and then in a micro second the other two were dropping hammers.

Phil saw the driver's gun recoil once, twice, three times and then Jewell's gun started going off. For a second it looked like nothing happened, but then the driver's legs started to buckled and he started down.

Phil had brought his gun to bear on the driver and was still pulling off shots as the driver and Jewell became engaged. You couldn't have told which gun was doing what there was a melee of gun fire and rounds flying all over the place.

As Jewell was dumping Benito, he

heard the car horn and knew the driver was out of the building. Jewell came up out of the Chrysler and turned to take on the driver. It was no longer a planned event, but had become an event of instinct each opponent responding and bringing to bear their weapons on the opposition.

Jewell saw the driver bringing his gun to bear on him and saw something hit the driver's lower left leg causing him to jerk down and to the right as the round hit home then the second round hit the driver high. Then he heard the driver's gun going off, his arm recoiling with each shot. It was strange, he knew he had been hit and was starting to return fire himself, but he heard another gun going off. He saw the first round hit home and they were not his and then in a heartbeat his rounds hit the driver and then several more rounds coming in from behind him hitting the driver. Phil, damn Phil was coming on strong.

Phil looked over at Jewell and could see immediately that something was wrong. He dove back into the car and slammed it into gear and pulled up by the rear bumper of the Chrysler. At the same time Jewell had turned and started to run to the car. He got in and Phil hit the gas and they were out on the street and heading back for the Mustang in just seconds.

Phil still had his gun sitting in his lap when he reached over to Jewell, "Jewell, you all right?"

Silence, Phil couldn't take his eyes off the road and he had to control his speed and action in order to avoid being observed or creating something that would draw people's attention to them. He concentrated on driving and getting back to the Mustang.

He knew damn well that Jewell had been hit the only problem was he did not know where or how serious it was. All he could do was get to the Mustang and do it in a manner that would not draw attention to them.

Twenty-five minutes later he was pulling in alongside the Mustang. He looked over at Jewell. His face was gray and he was holding his right leg. Phil reached over and felt the wetness on the upper part of the leg.

Phil pulled his hand back and leaned over, looking into Jewell eyes, "Jewell, how bad?"

Jewell sat up and looked back into Phil's eyes. "Bad enough, it's a through and through. Lots of bleeding, I'll need a doctor."

Phil was trying to think, "Yeah, but it's

271

a gunshot wound and they'll report it."

Jewell started shaking his head and looking at Phil. "No, they won't."

Phil was confused and scared by this time, "Why not?" He was almost begging Jewell for an answer.

Jewell jerked the door open and started getting out of the car. "Look, help me to the Mustang now."

Phil ran around the car and grabbed Jewell under the arms and literally carried him to the Mustang. Before he put him in, he had spread one of the plastic tarps out on the front seat and floor and set Jewell on it.

He then set the burn bomb in the stolen car and activated it, rolled one of the windows down half way, then got in the Mustang and headed for the park entrance. They cleared the park and were heading west when Jewell told Phil to go to a hardware store.

Hardware store, what the hell did he want to go to a hardware store now for anyway? Phil had no idea just what Jewell was thinking, but after two months of running with him Phil had learned that Jewell was always thinking and always had a plan. With that he headed for a hardware store.

Five minutes into their leaving the park

area the burn bomb went off with a whoosh and the car was engulfed in flames that spread through the whole of the car completely destroying it and its contents. By the time it was discovered and the fire department called and getting there, the car was totally destroyed. Nothing of value or evidential value was left.

Phil didn't question Jewell or hesitate. He found a hardware store and Jewell told him to go in and get a two-foot length of quarter inch re-bar. Phil didn't know what the hell he wanted the re-bar for, but went into the store, got the re-bar, and returned to the car.

Jewell had managed to get the holes plugged and the bleeding stopped before Phil got back. "All right, let's get out of here."

They drove another three blocks and Jewell had Phil pull into a closed business parking lot. Jewell then told Phil to get out of the car and take the re-bar and bend it leaving about eighteen inches on one side of the bend. Jewell then opened his door and had Phil hand him the re-bar. "Jewell, what the hell are you going to do? Damn-it man we need to get you medical attention and we don't have time for this."

Phil was completely puzzled by what

Jewell was doing until he took the bar and started to shove it into the hole in his thigh. It was an ugly mess. He tried twice to get the bar started into the hole, but it hung up on the pants the first time and then the entry hole the second time. He finally got it going and had to push with everything he had to get it to tear its way through the leg and out the other side. After he had pushed it all the way through the thigh and out the other side, he was spent.

Jewell couldn't keep from screaming, yet he mustered every ounce of strength he had and forced the re-bar through the wound. There was blood everywhere and if he did not bleed to death before Phil got him to the hospital that would be a miracle in itself.

When he finished, he sat there breathing as slowly as he could so that he could keep from passing out. "Damn that hurt, now get me to a hospital as soon as you can and keep within the speed limits, Oh and no red light running either."

Phil could hardly believe what he had just witnessed. A massive wave of nausea rolled over him and he almost passed out. "What the hell are you doing any way, for God's sake that's crazy?"

He was totally stunned and was finding

it hard to think, let alone keep from passing out. He was able to get it all together and then started looking for a hospital.

Jewell reached out with his bloody left hand and grabbed Phil by the shirt. "Don't you dare pass out on me, now relax, it's not hurting you, but it's damn near killing me. Now, take me to a hospital."

Jewell directed Phil to Joliet and they found a Physicians Immediate Care facility and Phil helped Jewell into the facility. They took him into an exam room and of course they asked what had happened.

Jewell told them that they had been looking over a possible investment sight and he stumbled and fell and landed on a piece of re-bar and it went through his leg. He looked at the nurse, "That damn thing is really hurting, could you give me something for it." She looked at him and shook her head.

"Sorry, but I can't do that until the doctor sees you. You may have lost too much blood and any kind of medication could be a real hazard to your life."

It seemed like hours before a doctor finally came in and looked at the mess lying on the table. "Gees man, how the hell did you do this?" Phil stepped up and told him what had happened and that Jewell was in some real pain right now and if the doctor could give him something for it.

The doctor said yes and asked the nurse to bring it in and administer it to him. When the drug hit Jewell, they could have picked him up by the re-bar and carried him out to the car. He had not a care in the world.

They extracted the re-bar from his leg and closed the wounds and bandaged him. He was provided with crutches and Phil paid the bill and they left. When they got in the car Phil pulled the plastic tarp out and rolled it up. He took a second smaller tarp and placed it under Jewell and they then returned to their apartment.

They got to the apartment some four hours after the hit and Jewell was finally down and relaxing. Phil turned on the television and it was full of the shoot out and death results.

"Benito Cipozzio, reputed mafia godfather, had been killed in a gun battle in front of the Homewood Pizza Parlor. His driver Anthony Carbon had been killed as well. The police had no leads or clues as of the time of the report.

"Over the years Mr. Cipozzio had been

referred to as the Godfather of the Cipozzio Mafia crime family. Most recently he was in the news concerning the matter of the death of his son Benjamin Cipozzio whose body was discovered in the State of Washington some four weeks after his disappearance. Benjamin was determined to have been killed after it was discovered there had been a gun battle in the bedroom at his personal residence. No suspects were identified or arrested in that case."

As they watched the news Phil finally turned to Jewell and asked. "Jewell, when you leaned into the car to do the job it looked like you said something to Benito, did you?"

By this time Jewell was doped and all his inhibitions were gone. "Yeah, I did."

Phil didn't know if he wanted to ask the next question, but he couldn't help himself. "What did you say?"

Jewell sat there. "Phil when I jerked the door open, he looked at me and his face went ashen. He said, "Jewell!"

At that point all the history between me, my family and Ben and Benito went through my mind. I hated that man, but I was also grateful to him for all the good things he did for me, but I knew that all that was now history and this was now and now was the time to end this thing.

I said to him, "Benito, Ben tried to kill me and I was fighting for my life. I knew you would never forgive me and you would see me dead no matter what Ben had done. I told him the only way out for you and me was to kill him. He called me a son-of-a-bitch and then I shot him three times."

Jewell then said. "Thanks to you honking the horn and opening up on the driver I was able to respond in time to stop Anthony. I realized that I was not the only one shooting at him. I saw the round coming in on him from the right and knew that you were backing me up and you did one hell of a job.

"He still got me, but it could have been worse. We did the job Phil and we both survived. Now we need to sit and wait. Things will start to hit the papers and airways in a couple of days. We'll know if it's over or not."

It was a big deal across the greater Chicago area and there were lots of stories in the paper about Benito and the family. There was speculation that it was a hit by one of the other families or possibly it was an ordered hit from New York or something like that. The stories just flew.

Three days later one of the television stations happened to find and interview Carl Sarcina a close friend of Benito. He was adamant that Benito was not a gangster and that someone must have tried to hold him up and killed him when they couldn't get him to cooperate. Jewell sat there watching the interview. A slight smile came across his face and he seemed to relax.

Phil immediately knew something big had just happened, he could read it in Jewell's face. "What? Jewell, what just happened?"

Jewell looked over at Phil and started to laugh. He couldn't stop and Phil just sat there watching him. Finally, Jewell regained control. "The new boss has told Carl to pull back and drop everything."

Phil was completely confused by this time. These Mafia guys were a strange bunch of characters. "What does that mean?"

By this time Jewell was completely relaxed and laying back with a smile that covered his whole face. "Phil, that means you can go back home and live-in peace."

Phil still had not realized that it was over. "Don't shit me on this Jewell."

Jewell waved his right hand and looked at him. "No, Phil, that's the truth. It's over.

New leadership has taken over in the family. They have confirmed that Benito had not been hit by any of the other families and that the matter is now closed.

"They will be burying him with full honors and all the family heads will be there. Carl has become the bodyguard for the new family boss and he likes that. He was loyal to Benito, but when he, Benito, had been killed that ended his loyalty. That's the way they are. It's a day-to-day existence and as each day changes the smart soldier rolls with the change."

All Phil could do is sit there and look at Jewell. "Well, I'll be damned."

He got up and walked into the bathroom, picked up the razor and started shaving the beard off. Jewell sat there watching him and then started to laugh. He laughed all the while Phil was shaving. Finally, when he finished Phil returned to the living room and sat down.

Phil just sat there like he was worn out. "Was that all that funny?"

Jewell, by this time was starting to think about tomorrow. Where he would be going and what he would be doing. "Phil, no, it wasn't your shaving, it was the look on

Benito's face when I opened the door. It never dawned on him that we would come after him. That's what was funny. He was too damn sure of himself.

"Like most of the self-righteous SOB's he thought he was untouchable. He was a tyrant and used to having people grovel at his feet. He was on top so long that he thought no one would dare touch him no matter the reason.

"The reason this whole thing happened in the first place was his attitude toward life and those under him. It rubbed off on Ben and Ben was finally starting to act the same way. That came through that morning while we were talking on the phone.

"These people are all the same. They bully you and then when that doesn't work, they'll glad hand you, and when you're not expecting it, they have you killed. As soon as Ben started to get friendly with me, after treating me the way he had I knew I was now a marked man.

"It's an ego thing with them. Do as I say and if you don't I lose face and when I lose face it is harder for me to keep control, so if I lose face, you die. I was sure when I left home that morning that Ben planned on me never returning.

"I knew that when I got to the house Ben had to be in one of three places. If he was in his den then all was well. If he was on the veranda then it was all right as well. But when he told me he was in his bedroom I knew that the trap had been set and it was an ambush. That's exactly what it was and I defended myself."

It was over, yet it was not over. Phil still had to go home and there were other issues that he would need to deal with when he got there, but they were nothing compared to what he had gone through.

Finally, Phil sat back and just looked at the television. He had started out on his yearly vacation trip and ended up in Chicago. He had been chased over two-thirds of the country and was involved in four-gun fights. He had gone from a quiet no name lifestyle to being a partner with a professional hit man. All that in just a couple of months' times.

Yes, he was glad it was over and he could start to look forward to getting back to a normal life. The major issue for him now was what a normal life really was for him.

He felt spent. There was no energy left in him. He wanted to sit there and let time slide by, and not commit to anything other than relaxing and leaving the world to itself for a little while. Damn, it was over, so he thought.

Chapter Eleven

BACK TO THE OLD GRIND

Phil stayed with Jewell until the heat settled down and everything appeared to be back to normal. Jewell had checked with several friends and learned that the hit had been rescinded and that he could relax. It was over and everything was back to status quo. Benito would be cast into history and it would be business as usual for the family and its new Godfather.

Jewell new better and started to make plans to leave the Chicago area. After all, he had nothing left in the place. His home had been burned and anything else he had been involved with was no long available to him.

There was no place for him here.

Sunday morning, five weeks after the hit, Phil walked out to the living room. Jewell was sitting there reading the paper. Phil was feeling rested and energized. It had been the first good sleep he had had in weeks. "Well, I think I'll start heading back home today. I don't know about you but I really do want to get back and reclaim my life."

The days following the successful action had been needed for Jewell's wound, which had been treated and cared for by Phil, was healed enough so that he could get along on his own.

Jewell had been reading the morning paper and watching the television news when Phil came out, he looked up, "Really, this soon. I would think that you would want to relax for a few more days."

Phil walked over and picked up one of the morning papers and was skimming over the front page. "Yeah, I have to go home and see if I still have a job."

Jewell adjusted his position in his chair. "Think you do?"

Turning and walking toward the kitchen Phil tossed the paper on the table and said, over his shoulder. "I sure as hell hope so."

Jewell, almost as an afterthought asked, "Have you called David lately."

Phil stopped and leaned back into the living room. "Gees, no I haven't.

Jewell took a hand and ran it through his hair. "Well maybe you need to wait until you talk to him before taking off. One more day won't make any difference one way or the other."

Things had been so crazy these last few days and weeks and then with the shoot out and Jewell's injury he had forgot about contacting David. "Yeah, you're right I'll hang around until tomorrow after I talk to David."

Jewell sat up, looked at Phil. "Meanwhile, how about we take a ride."

"Take a ride!" That is not a good thing one wants to hear from someone with Jewell's background. Phil looked at Jewell and said cautiously, "Where to?"

His demeanor had changed and he was not the intense and targeting Jewell he had been the days before, "Oh, a place."

All the warning bells were going off in Phil head. *No, he promised me that no harm would come to me if he could help it.* "Jewell, what are you up to?"

Jewell could see the shadow of concern move across Phil's face and he smiled. "Not much, I just had an idea and thought you may want to go along."

By now Phil was more than a little concerned and looked at him again. Then it hit him, hell, if he wanted me dead, he would have done it that day at the shootout. "What the hell, sure, let's go?"

Jewell was still smiling when Phil finally made up his mind. He stood up, picked up the keys to the Mustang, walked over and picked up a suitcase, opened the door. Phil looked at the suitcase and then at Jewell. "What the hell are you up to anyway?" There was a degree of strain in Phil's voice.

Jewell continued to smile that goofy 'I know something you don't know.' Smile and walked out the door. Phil followed him, closing and locking the door behind him. They were walking out the front of the building when Phil reached out and grabbed Jewell by his left shoulder. "Hold up Jewell, what's this about and what's the suitcase for?"

Jewell stopped and turned and told Phil. "Look, I have something I need to show you and I can't go into it until we are there. So just trust me and let's go."

They went to the Mustang and Jewell got in the driver's side and Phil the passenger side. They headed south from their apartment. A short time later as they crossed the Illinois and Indiana line Phil was beginning to get nervous, again.

Jewell felt it and looked at Phil. This time he took pity on Phil and told him. "Relax, this is not a bad thing, but I don't want to tell you about it right now. Just sit tight and enjoy the trip."

Assurances like that are common place for people in Jewell's area or field of work. Phil was still uneasy, "Where we going?"

Jewell decided to give the guy at least something to ease his mind. "We're going to Indianapolis Phil and will probably be there two or three days. After that you can be on your way and I'll give you the Mustang as well."

It was about two hundred miles from their apartment to Indianapolis. They made it in good time and found a nice motel and settled in for the night. Jewell was still keeping quiet about their reason for being there and Phil still had that gut feeling that anything could happen at any time.

The next morning, they got up had breakfast and went out and got into the Mustang and headed into town. This was unusual in that they had always skirted the cities preferring to stay outside those high-risk areas.

That told Phil that Jewell was relaxed and not worried about any action from the mob. Once downtown, Jewell went into the financial district and stopped at one of the largest banks in the city. They sat in the parking lot and Jewell reached into his pocket and pulled out a small envelope.

Jewell sat there turning that envelope over in his hand, just looking at it. He then turned to Phil. "Remember when I was leaning into the car talking to Benito just before I gave it to him?"

"Yes." Answered Phil.

Jewell kept turning the envelope over and over in his hand and looking at it. "Well, I was also searching him. He always carried this small envelope in his shirt pocket. I never, ever saw him without this envelope.

"When I opened it up it had a key and the name of three banks on a small piece of paper. By each bank name was a number. As I thought about it, I determined that the key was a bank safety deposit box key and that the banks listed were the banks he had a safety deposit box in. The single key puzzled me for a time and then I realized he had all three boxes in the three different banks keyed to the same key. On the back of the piece of paper was a single word "Genevieve".

"I have a hunch about that word and it came to me that it was a password and that brought me back to the three boxes. So, let's go in and see what box number one is all about." By this time Phil was more than interested, he was downright eager.

Damn this was exciting and he was going to be in on the bottom floor of whatever was going on. Any worry about Jewell being a mobster had vanished and he was now engrossed with the idea that the old man had kept safety deposit boxes in three separate banks in Indianapolis.

They walked inside the bank and looked around. It was not unlike most banks however; this one was big and well used by the residents of Indianapolis. They went to the safe deposit box desk and registered for the box number on the papers, provided the password and then, were taken to see that box.

The clerk did her thing and took them

290

back into the vault and had them enter a small room and left them there. A few minutes later she was back with a large deposit box on a rolling table.

The two of them stood there looking at the box, Phil looked at Jewell and asked, "Well. Are we going to open it?"

Jewell turned the box facing them and lifted the lid.

They both stood there looking into the box. Jewell sat back and placed his hands on the table, on both sides of the box. Phil leaned forward and over the box.

Both men were clearly puzzled and pleased with what they were looking at. Phil's mind shot back to that day so long ago when he first met Jewell, and the time he learned who Jewell was and what was going on in his life. He saw the police officer as the gunman shot him down and then thought about his wife and family. Each and every event charged across his mind as he looked into that box and realized what was there.

Jewell was doing the same thing, reliving his encounter with Ben and the gun fight that he survived. His going west and taking Ben with him and then burying him in Washington State and eventually meeting Phil and taking him on this once in a lifetime thrill ride across the country. That box was the culmination of all that the two of them had gone through and now it was theirs.

The box was full top to bottom with five hundred-dollar bills all neatly wrapped in stacks of one hundred thousand dollars. Well, Jewell guessed each bundle had that much in it.

The two of them stood there, not quite knowing what to do and yet wanting so much to reach in and grab a handful.

Jewell just shook his head, "That sly old man. That no-good double-crossing son-of-a-bitch, he was padding his future and no one knew about it. If anyone in the family had known about this that old fart would have been dead a long time ago.

"That two-faced greedy animal was playing a game that would have resulted in half the family being killed if the big guys in New York had figured this out."

Phil reached out and ran his hand over the top of the bills. "How much do you think is in there?"

Jewell had no idea and yet needed to say something, because he wanted an idea as well. "I would say around five million and if the other two banks have the same thing, my friend we are just plain stinking rich."

The first thing they had to do was regain their composure and calm down. This was not the time to draw attention to them, they needed to get the money packed and get the hell out of there. They packed the money into a bank bag and left the bank and drove to the next one.

The anticipation was almost unbearable at that point. Plain logic told them that if the first bank had that much money in the box, then the other two would too. They almost didn't want to think about it and if it was true then man did, they have a future.

When they got to the second bank, they both sat there looking across the parking lot at the front entrance of the bank. There was nothing wrong with their being there. They had the key and the password and the number and so the money was theirs.

The second bank was the same thing. They had parked, walked in and were taken to a room and a box delivered to them, the same exact size as the first one. When opened they saw the same contents and quickly removed them and left the bank. Now they had around ten million dollars in the Mustang and were getting a little nervous about leaving that much money in the trunk by itself.

At the next bank they planned on parking as close to the front door as possible so that they would not be that far away and so that the presence of a lot of people coming and going from the bank would make any wood-be prowler think twice before trying to enter the Mustang.

They still needed to enter the bank and go through the same process as they had with the other two banks. After the third bank stop and finding the same results, they headed back to their motel. They had three bank bags in the trunk, each one holding around five million dollars. Phil was thinking this is just plain crazy. How the hell one man could set something like this up anyway. He had to have done it years ago and then made periodic trips down here on his own to add more to it.

Or, maybe he put it all in the banks in one big load and then left it there as a retirement, get-a-way fund. No matter what his mental agenda was he had left a huge amount of money sitting in one spot for a long time.

Once in their room they set the money out on the table top and just looked at it, God that was a big pile of money. Phil looked over at Jewell, "How much is there?"

Jewell looked back; "I think it's a lot more than fifteen million."

They just sat there. Phil's mind raced back through the past few months, going over the killings, the running, and the ending of their ride. All he could do was shake his head. Jewell was just staring at the pile, not saying nor doing anything. Then he said. "That my friend is the future for us."

Almost at the same time both reached into the pile and started pulling bundles of bills out and breaking them open. It took hours, but they were able to count the money and eventually came up with a grand total of twenty-four million dollars.

It was fair to say that they were both truly shocked at the amount of money. Phil had never in his life seen that much money in one place. Jewell on the other hand had seen a lot of money from time to time, but nothing to match this.

He finally was able to get his voice back. He then said. "That my dear Phil is payday for all that has happened to you over the past few months. Twelve million should take you a long way."

Phil's mouth dropped open. Jewell was going to share it equally with him, he was keeping his word. He then said, "Twelve million frigging dollars. That's a retirement fund of six hundred thousand a year for life. Wow, I could go anywhere and do anything."

Jewell laughed. "That's all up to you Phil. Your first problem is figuring out how you're going to carry it and how you're going to get it into a bank without bringing the government down on you."

Phil hadn't thought of that and was sitting there trying to determine just how he would do that. "Jewell, what are you going to do?"

Jewell sat back and thought for a few minutes and then said. "I'm heading for the coast. I'm going to find me a nice town and settle down by the ocean so that I can go out and watch it any time I want.

"On the way out there, I am going to stop in a number of cities and lease safety deposit boxes at a couple of banks in each city. Then place a million in each and work the movement of that money around when I find a permanent place to live."

Phil thought about that and decided that was what he would be doing as well. "Well

296

then, after we talk to David, what say we travel together back out to the coast?"

Jewell nodded his head. "That my friend sounds great."

Once they had made the decision to head west, they sat there looking at the money. They had hunted down the animal that had been the cause of all their grief over the past couple of months. After that they discovered all this money, and after all those hard times that old fart was going to pay them for all their work.

They packed the money back into the bank bags, checked out of the motel and returned to the Chicago area apartment. When they arrived, they moved the money into the apartment and Phil made that call to me.

"Hi David."

I sounded like and was a little surprised. "Phil, you, all right?"

Phil paused a moment and then said. "That my dear friend is a positively yes answer.

You could hear the relief in my voice. "Is everything all right back there?"

Phil took his time and told me. "Yes, it is. In fact, I'll be heading back that way tomorrow, anything going on there David?

I was trying to remain professional, but you could feel and hear the edge in my voice. "Yes, there is. The police want to talk to you. I advised them that I had no idea where you were, but that as soon as I heard from you, I would tell you. Phil, they found your car at the scene of a police officer's shooting. They want to talk to you really bad."

Phil knew that this would eventually catch up with him. "All right David, you can call them back and tell them that I'm on my way home and when I get there I'll come in and talk with them. I'll want you with me also."

I relaxed a little. "No problem, Phil. How long will you be? Oh, and can you fill me in on what was going on with your car please?"

Phil thought for a few seconds and then said. "David, as you know, Jewell and I were traveling through that part of Oregon and had stopped at a restaurant for dinner. We were there maybe an hour and a half and as we were leaving, we saw these two guys in the lot. We managed to avoid them, but the next day as we were heading out, they caught up with us and stopped at the same art gallery where I had stopped. I thought that they were satisfied with my answers when the one guy talked to me in the gallery. We left town and headed south.

It turns out they had us figured and followed us out of town. We saw them stop by a police car and then the police car came after us with these two guys in a black Cad following the officer. I have no idea what they said to that officer but whatever it was it was believable enough to cause the officer to pursue and stop us.

We pulled off the main highway and stopped in a wide spot on that road. The Cad came around us and at that moment the two got out. The driver went right at the officer and killed him on the spot. It was at that time the Jewell cut them down and we took their car and left.

We couldn't be taken in by the police at that time. The mob would know it was us and we would have been dead. All the way across the country we fought for our lives with each attack. It finally ended in Chicago, and with that I will be able to return home safe and alive thanks to Jewell. As far as I'm concerned, every bit of that situation where the officer was killed was a self-defense issue."

I thought about what Phil had said and then responded. "All right Phil based on what you just told me and what the police have told me, it was a clear case of self-defense. I'll contact them and fill them in and we'll make a determination as to whether we need to meet with them."

"Look, David, not only were the mob hunting us but the police were hunting us in regards to the Chicago thing and we felt that we couldn't get involved with them at that time. We just bought a car and cleared out."

I sat there thinking for a few seconds and nothing more became apparent. "All right Phil, I'll let them know."

Phil would have a week plus to think everything over and prepare himself for any meeting with the police. If all went well, he would not need to do that. "Thanks David. See you in a week or so."

That car, Jewell was right about it. It kept coming back and haunting him. He knew that they were more than just a little interested in what took place on the country road in southwestern Oregon and he would have to be careful when telling his story.

The rule was to keep it short and simple and stay with the truth, that way it was easier to remember. They had the guys that killed the officer, but they wanted to know who killed those guys. If he kept it simple that would satisfy them.

When they cleared out of the apartment, they packed everything they had including garbage and junk, taking everything. Last they packed their bags and stuffed them into the Mustang and prepared to leave town going west the next morning.

That evening they went out for a good dinner and then the next morning they headed for St. Louis. When they got into St. Louis the two of them would then go to nearby, but separate banks, and open their first account and safety deposit box. Each one opened an account and deposited one million dollars in each of their respective safety deposit boxes. They also made small deposits into their active accounts. They then would head west targeting their next bank location.

Once they arrived at the next large city, they would then locate two more banks and open new accounts and make the same size safety deposit box deposits and a small deposit in their active accounts. This would continue on through several cities and a total of eleven banks for each one across the county before all the monies were deposited.

So, at the end of the first day out they had stopped and made deposits in three cities. This drive was going to be much smoother and less challenging than the ride out. It would still require them to drive in a zigzag pattern across the country, making stops in all the larger cities to make their deposits. Later on, they would consolidate their deposits in the area where they individually settled down.

In a few short weeks they should have everything closed out and life should be back to normal. After all, with all the problems old Benito brought them, it was only right that they receive some kind of compensation for all the hard work and hard times they had.

A week and a half later, as they came into the Seattle area on Interstate 90, they turned north to Everett and went looking for a new car lot.

Jewell decided that he wanted a new Cadillac CTS. He would be leaving Phil in a short time and he decided to go in style. His target was the Oregon coast and the Pacific Ocean. He had no idea as to what he was going to do with his life from then on. After all a guy had to have something to pass the time, he would figure that out in due time. All that was important now was finding a place and settling in, he was now retired.

Once the car was in Jewell's hand he looked over at Phil, "Hey, don't be a stranger. Come on down and see me from time to time. I'll even treat you for your cost to come down, couldn't be that much unless you decide to travel in style."

Phil stood there looking at Jewel and thinking back to that day in the rest area parking lot when this stranger walked up to him and asked for a ride. That seemed like a thousand years ago and a lot of blood and sweat. "Same goes for you Jewell."

As a result of random selection, Jewell had run into this computer geek that he determined was his ride to safety. It had been many weeks ago and now he was looking at and saying good bye to probably the best partner he had ever worked with. "All right, anyway, thanks you were a great partner."

Then it came to Phil and he turned back to Jewell. "Hey, are you done contracting now? I mean is there a possibility that you may get back into the business anytime in the future? You know there may be others outside the mob that could use your skills from time to time."

When Jewell heard that he sat back against his new car and looked at the ground. "Yah knows Phil, I'm status-non-gratis now with that part of the world, so I doubt if I'll ever be called again, so, to answer your question probably not. Then on the other hand you may be right about others wanting my services, which could happen. Why do you ask?"

Phil walked up to him and turned and leaned back against his new car. "Well, I was thinking, if ever you get back into that business again and need a partner, I think I'll probably be available. Not that I want to get into that line of work, but I would hate to see you have to work one on your own."

Jewell's mouth dropped open. "Why Phil, I didn't think you were partial to that kind of work? But, let me say this. If I do get back into contracting, and I doubt if I ever will, I would have no problem with you partnering up with me."

Phil stood back up. "Really, you would work with me again. You think I'm that good?"

Jewell reached out and put his hand on Phil's shoulder. "Yeah, I would work with you again. Not because I think your that good, but because I would need a shield from time to time. Now, I have to leave, we'll get together in a few months and talk things over. Take care and keep the faith man.

"Oh, by the way, if you need any help on that issue with the police let me know and I'll see what I can do to help out. Don't know how much help I would be, but I could do something."

Phil was nodding his head. "No, I think that maybe it is better if you stay out of that and let David and I work this out. I really think it will work out just fine."

"All right Phil whatever you want." Jewell replied. "Be in good health and let me know how things work out, good luck."

Phil stepped away from the car and watched as Jewell got into the driver's seat and started the motor. Just then Phil called out. "You too Jewell. Oh Jewell?"

Jewell looked out the window, "Yeah."

Phil smiled. "It's you eighteen me six"

Jewell laughed, waved and drove off.